SOMEWHERE
IN THE NIGHT

Also by Jeffrey N. McMahan

VAMPIRES
ANONYMOUS

SOMEWHERE IN THE NIGHT

Eight Gay Tales of the Supernatural

by Jeffrey N. McMahan

alyson
books

LOS ANGELES • NEW YORK

Manufactured in the United States of America.
Printed on acid-free paper.

This trade paperback original is published by Alyson Publications Inc.,
P.O. Box 4371, Los Angeles, California 90078-4371.
Distribution in the United Kingdom by Turnaround Publisher Services Ltd.,
Unit 3 Olympia Trading Estate, Coburg Road, Wood Green,
London N22 6TZ, England.

First edition: October 1989
Second edition: October 1997

01 00 99 98 97   10 9 8 7 6 5 4 3 2 1

ISBN 1-55583-432-9

Cover design by Bruce Zinda.

To Chris…
one you can read in the proper form…

CONTENTS

Special thanks to...

Third Street Writers Group, a clutch of fun, witty, intelligent, dedicated, and helpful writers who played important roles in the shaping and fine tuning of these stories — Monserrat Fontes, Karen Sandler, Janet Gregory, Gerry Citrin, the late Naomi Sloan, and especially Katherine V. Forrest.

Kathy, thanks eternal for that good swift kick in the ever-popular area. Without your loving shove, this book would be gathering dust and nicotine stains with the rest.

I also want to acknowledge and thank the proprietors and employees of El Carmen Café, Third Street, Los Angeles — particularly Paul, Tony, Rosa, Lorenzo, Leo, Lupe, Dena, Patricia, and, a flash from the past, Geri — for allowing the group to gather and disrupt twice a month.

Set up a double strawberry margarita, my favorite — thanks!

In loving memory of Naomi...
our elegance and our dignity...
without you, we will never be as good

INTRODUCTION

*I*magine the darkness, that unknowable place we've been taught to fear. The Dark — a planet, a universe. A condition so terrifying that even dark people are made the object of our loathing. Imagine the night, your bedroom at 3 A.M., or the secret you've never told anyone. Horror stories have always lived in the dark, in those fearsome places we've been taught to hate. Yet writers are continually drawn to them. Whether it's Edgar Allan Poe, Edith Wharton, or Stephen King, writers have always sought out the world living in that darkness.

Perhaps it is their ability to see the dark as full of possibility, a place where adventure can be found. In the dark these writers discover something else to know, to explore. With the tendency to sexual (in addition to special) experimentation frequently found in fantasy fiction, queer writers have been drawn naturally to the world of speculative fiction. Early lesbian feminist literature featured several utopian gynocracy novels, such as Sally Gearhart's *Wanderground* and Joanna Russ's *The Female Man*, both of which became cultural icons. Clive Barker has found a niche in mainstream horror that includes an international audience.

Jeffrey N. McMahan joins these writers in the effort to make the genre his own. Reaching deeply into the frightening places — both mythological and emotional — McMahan creates compelling tales of contemporary life. Yet the world he depicts is the underbelly of an Absolut ad; it's the white gay world turned inside out, viscera exposed, dripping blood on the fashionable carpet.

What McMahan proves, as others have before him, is that any genre can be suitable for examining our lives, for telling a good story. In *Somewhere in the Night,* he conjures up wry vampires, vengeful ghosts, and cannibalistic goblins, investing each story with an affecting blend of terror, love, and sensuality. The cruelty of homophobia, xenophobia, and class envy are perfect elements for a horror story. McMahan imagines the festering wounds caused by those emotions and the tragedy they unleash in "The Dark Red Day." From the moment the main character, Richard, pulls into the gas station on the edge of his hometown, the anxiety of violence wafts from the page. It's a violence that many of us can envision, that some of us have fled. Despite the aura of dread hanging over his visit, Richard tries to reclaim love but instead comes face-to-face with the roiling rage of the town he's left behind. The complexities of home, love, and family make that renewal disastrous. And, as with much of

McMahan's work, the underlying sadness of loss that cannot be avoided sits firmly at the center of the fiery resolution.

McMahan's work is not without its delights of the body, even when the characters are looking over their shoulders. A natural sensuality hums through his stories: "the quiet rasp of his faint whiskers" on another man's face; the secret of desire that "crackles like a fragile thread of lightning...." The sensual moments are made even more evocative and urgent by the horror that surrounds them.

Another unexpected and effective element of McMahan's writing is his sense of humor. Woefully lacking in much of fantasy fiction, humor allows the reader to enter dark places with ease. McMahan has a sharp wit that he uses much as Joanna Russ does in some of her short stories. Self-conscious witticisms help define the characters and invite the reader to come closer to an edge otherwise too forbidding. A humorous tone propels the "Cruising With Andrew" stories — his dapper gay vampire has yet to perfect dressing without a mirror — leading us handily to the core of vampire life. When Andrew faces the night alone, he ponders the power to decide who might join him in eternal life. Unlike the casual cruelty practiced by many traditional vampires, the decision looms large for Andrew: Who is the right one to bring over into vampire life, and who would be a disastrous mistake? It's a dilemma that follows Andrew like a conscious being, haunting his steps. There are no guidelines, so he, like most of us, must rely on his instincts, on his judgment of the potential for good and evil. It's an irony not lost on McMahan or on Andrew, who knows his own limitations, preternatural though they may be."Ten minutes of unconquerable dilemma is more of an eternity than even I wish to face," Andrew remarks to himself. With that dilemma the vampire must face its darknesses.

In this collection Jeffrey McMahan has created a world full of the terrors of both the known and the unknown. Being afraid is one of the signs we're still alive. Step into the beautiful dark.

Jewelle L. Gomez
San Francisco, 1997

TWO-FACED JOHNNY

*T*errific!

Just terrific!

Halloween just around the corner and not a party in sight.

Not at all like last year. Such a party! Scads of people — huge variety of costumes. Food, drink, thrills and chills.

Of course, some people got too drunk and went out of control.

I won't mention any names.

He knows who he is.

Not a party in sight.

Gots, what a bummer.

Name's Johnny, by the way. Nice to meet ya.

I'd like to tell you what I look like, but being the scrawler that I am, I know the rules of first person. It is not possible to convincingly work in one's description without displaying amateur awkwardness. For example:

"I wake up at nine — late as usual — and stagger into the bathroom. Biceps bulging, I grip the cool porcelain sink and lean toward the mirror. My blond hair certainly is straight today — like yesterday. What a surprise! My blue eyes are almost transparent in the fluorescent bathroom light. . . ."

Let us grasp seriousness and reality by the hand. Nobody does that!

But I want you to know what I look like.

Toss caution to the clichéd wind, I say. I don't need a mirror; I know exactly what I look like — from memory.

My hair is dark brown, almost black; short at the sides and back, long and full, reaching toward the sky on top. My eyes are big and brown, my nose straight. My mouth is wide, the lips just thick and (for a man) shapely enough to make you look twice and — well hell, the mouth is seductive. Why beat around the bush?

Five ten and one hundred thirty pounds. (The doctor says I'm too thin; eat more. What a quack!) Thirty years old with a fourteen-year-old's body. Well, not all of it. Some people have commented that certain assets are grand beyond the mastery of even someone my age. Fools! Stories I could tell—

But I digress.

Halloween.

Gots, but I love Halloween. My favorite of all holidays.

At what other time of year can I take this gorgeous face and child body and deform both beyond recognition of even Dear Old Mom.

Halloween.

All Hallow's Eve.

Trick or treat.

And not a bloody party in sight!

O

Oh, great! The phone. Don't people realize I'm trying to have a conversation here? In all likelihood it's Robert. I'd wager a week's pay that it's Robert.

Coming! Coming!

Revenge is mine, saith Johnny.

Robert is the one who got drunk and went out of control at last year's Halloween party.

"Hello, Robert."

"Get dressed."

"I am dressed."

"No, dunce, *dressed*."

"You found a party!"

"Not exactly. I thought we'd cruise until we found one that looks like it's jumpin'."

"Robert, I'm not spending three hours with latex and paint on the slim chance—"

"I'll be there at eight. Be ready or sit at home and talk to yourself."

Click and buzzzzzzz.

I stare at the receiver. Talk to myself indeed. You're listening, right?

All right. Time — what's the time? Half past five. That's only two and a half hours to get ready. Damn, shit — and a string of curses I won't bore you with.

It's a good thing I've already designed this year's get-up. Just in case a party decided to happen.

O

Biceps bulging, I grip the cool porcelain sink and lean toward the bathroom mirror.

Would I lie to you?

Seven forty-five and I'm ready. A record.

Am I a sight! I hope Robert's wearing brown pants because he's going to soil them when he sees me.

My hair has receded three inches and stands in gray and white spikes. My brow is high and hangs hairless over a bumpily ridged, off-center nose with flaring nostrils. With the help of contact lenses I swiped from the studio where I work, my eyes have gone to bloodshot cataracts. My mouth is even wider, the lips thicker. Now people will stare in revulsion at the seeping cracks and boils.

My skin from the top of my forehead to the soles of my feet — I leave no stone unturned or patch uncovered — is translucent, ultra-pale green with tiny red blood vessels showing through. My shoulders slump, my chest and stomach are sunken; my spine is ridged and twisted. My hands and feet are age-coarsened, the nails broken. The ultimate, finishing touch — purple cankers riddle my entire body.

The wonders of modern Halloween make-up! Aren't we all thrilled that someone finally realized that Halloween is for adults and not for brats?

If Robert doesn't find a party to show me off at, I'll kill him and eat him, toes, fingers, and all, for supper.

At midnight. Of course.

O

The doorbell!

Robert is irritatingly punctual.

"Just a minute!"

"Open up or I'll leave without you!"

"I'll slaughter you, Robert! By Gots, I swear I'll have you limb from limb!"

"Promises. . . ."

Robert is a cretin.

I'm naked, don't ya know. Spent fifteen minutes admiring my skills with latex and paint in total ozone state of mind.

Dash to the door.

"Promise to wait thirty seconds after I unlock the door."

Anxiously, I await his response. He mustn't see me without the rest of my get-up. Effect, ya know.

He's taking too long to answer. He's not going to wait.

Carefully — ohsoverycarefully — I unlock the door.

And race for the bedroom.

The door crashes against the wall.

"I see a purple-cankered green tushie, Johnny boy!"

Robert has no class.

But I'm safely locked in my bedroom. The rest of my costume is laid out on the bed — sheer dark-gray hooded cloak, black Roman sandals, black jock strap (I dyed it myself) with knee-length tatters sewn to the waistband.

Robert isn't the only one who'll see purple-cankered green tushie this Halloween.

"You have three minutes, Johnny boy, then I cruise without you," in his most sing-songy falsetto.

Swiftly, but without smearing any make-up, I don the rest of my attire. The hood of the cloak sits perfectly atop the gray and white spikes and drapes over my face to my chest. I pull the cloak around me, turn off the light, throw back the door.

Robert is considerate.

He has dimmed the lights to give me full advantage for the revelation. Through the sheer gray hood, the living room and Robert are shrouded in graveyard murkiness.

"Not the cape again," Robert moans. "You used it last year—"

With dramatic flourish, I throw back the hood and fling open my cloak.

Robert screams.

I am a success.

O

Robert is a clown.

Cute but still clown, in or out of costume.

And sexy. No balloon clown costume for Robert. Bikini briefs; baubled, pointed hat. The rest of his sinewy muscles are painted in orange, blue, red, and yellow stripes and polka dots.

Gots, beneath the paint—

Robert's body is twenty even if he's a decade older.

I figure, put a fourteen-year-old's body and a twenty-year-old's body together and you surpass both our ages, and that's plenty—

But, again, I digress.

Robert is still mortified by my make-up and costume.

"God, Johnny boy, you're grotesque."

I grimace and bow to his praises.

"Eeyuck!" Robert backs away.

Oh, yes, I've covered my perfect white teeth with rows of yellow and black.

"You have got to get a picture of this one, Robert — and this year, take off the lens cap."

O

Thirty minutes on the road and not even a glimpse of a party.

Robert is jovial with the hunt.

I grow impatient and pray the cankers on my ass haven't smeared.

"There's one!" Robert whips the car in a life-threatening

U-turn and parks. He grins ear-to-ear and his teeth meld with his exaggerated clown-white mouth.

I wonder at Robert's party radar. Other than the cars parked in the driveway, the house exhibits no signs of festivities. The light behind the windows is dull; distorted shadows creep across the glass.

"Go check it out," I order/suggest.

"Me?"

"This was your idea."

"All right. Don't chomp your teeth to a froth." Giggling in delight of himself, he jumps out of the car and runs to look in the windows.

There's no sound — no music, no voices — coming from that house.

This street sure is quiet. No light in any other house; no porch lights on.

I wait for Robert in silence — how long?

No cars drive past.

I can't see Robert at the house. How could I miss a half-naked orange-blue-red-and-yellow-striped-and-polka-dotted man in a purple mop-head wig?

Maybe he went around back.

"Aren't you coming in to join us?"

I jump, bang my knee on the dashboard.

I strangle a scream.

A women is leaning into the passenger window of Robert's car.

And she's wearing *my costume*.

O

There is music, a slow throbbing bass that underscores high-pitched, staccato shrieks.

Men and women cavort around the large living room and stroll about the patio and circle the pool out back.

Such mixed fare is hardly what I had in mind, but we can start here, then—

Now just a bloody minute! Is it just the lighting or is this a bizarre case of Halloween make-up espionage? All — and I mean all — of these people are wearing my costume!

Red-veined, translucent green skin. Purple cankers and seeping boils. Gray and white spiked hair.

Even black-dyed jock straps.

No — shredded loin cloths. Smartasses.

Dark-gray sheer hooded cloaks hang on pegs by the door.

"Robert — where's Robert?" I ask of the woman standing close behind me.

"Robert?" She is perplexed. Then a flame glows behind her cataract eyes. "Oh — the clown." A smile of yellowed fangs — longer than mine, the bitch. She places a hand — a damned hot hand — on my shoulder. "Out by the pool, I would imagine."

Good. I'll just mosey out to the patio, find Robert — he should stand out like a rose in a brier patch in this crowd — hook a hand in the waist of his bikini, and drag him the hell out of here.

The woman presses against me — scorching through my cloak — and propels me into the room.

"Would you like a drink?"

"I really think—"

"But it's *fresh!*"

We cross toward the bar. Everyone turns and grimaces; burning bodies brush against mine.

"Can I take your wrap?" she asks.

"No. I'm a bit chilled—"

"Really?" The perplexity again. "A fresh glass for our new arrival," she says to the hulking mass behind the bar. She leers at me. "That will warm you up."

Someone lifts the back of my cloak. A firebrand caresses my ass.

"Ooo!"

I turn — Robert!

Wrong! Robert, even as a clown, out-looks this babe.

"Such a tushie," my second new friend jibes. Does she have a thousand hands and must she burn every inch of me with them? "Where'd you find this cutie?"

"Sitting outside in his car," my first new friend replies. She forces a glass of luminescent red punch into my hand. "Wall flower."

"Ooo, I like shy types," says the second.

I gulp at my drink in nervous desperation. Gots, but this drink is sweet!

"He wants to see Robert," says the first.

"Robert?"

"The *clown*."

"Ooo! Out at the barbecue!" A long, wasted, purple-cankered arm swings toward the patio doors.

I follow a gnarled index finger to a cluster of men and women chatting around the smoking barbecue pit.

Robert is tall, but I see no purple mop head above the crowd.

My two friends link their lava arms in mine and lead me outside.

I stumble. That drink went straight to my head. I gulp some more and almost choke on the sweetness.

The aroma of the barbecue hits me. Pungent, stinging my nostrils. I am reminded of Robert's aftershave.

The crowd around the barbecue pit turns to greet us.

"We've come to see Robert," my friends say in unison. "The clown."

"Aah!" says the crowd, and they step aside.

I don't know which part I see first, which part I recognize last. But Robert, so carefully sliced and diced, should be done in a few minutes.

Except his head — whole — shish-kebabbed through the ears. That'll take a bit longer.

O

Robert is dinner.

I scramble backward, collide with the bartender.

He smacks his lips. "Smells terrific!"

"What's wrong with you people?" I shriek.

People?

Get me out of here.

I head for the front door through the mass of hot bodies in my make-up.

Make-up?

"Where ya goin', Johnny?" My friends clutch at my arms.

"Out! Home!" I struggle free.

"But it's *early*! You haven't eaten."

"Look, I gotta go." I back across the living room, banging into furniture, tripping over people. "I'm not one of your crowd. I crashed your party. I should go."

"Sure you're one of us. Just look in the mirror."

I slam into a wall, wheel around to a full-length mirror.

Green translucent skin riddled with purple cankers.

Bloodshot, glowing cataract eyes.

High, bulging brow.

Swollen, cracked lips.

Gots, but I do look like one of them.

My ragged-nailed fingers fumble at my face.

"No. See. Mistake. Just a mistake."

But the make-up won't come off; it's grown into my skin.

I try to mat down the gray and white spikes. They spring pointily back.

Wait — here's a loose piece.

That hurts!

I'm bleeding. I tore off part of my bottom lip.

Reflected in that mirror, they all gape at me. All those hideous people that copied my make-up.

"What are you doing?" my second friend asks. "You'll hurt yourself."

"Mistake! This isn't my skin. My skin is smooth, white, unblemished. This isn't my face. My eyes are clear and brown, my nose is perfectly straight, my mouth—"

"Calm down," she says, those hot hands on my shoulder.

And her touch cools on my flesh, relaxes me.

I stop tearing at the make-up that is no longer make-up. My fingers trace the ridge of my brow, skim over my high forehead to the gray and white spikes of my hair. I carefully straighten a spike that has begun to droop.

I *have* hurt myself. I gingerly touch my bottom lip. I'm going to have a scar.

I turn from the mirror to my hostess and gathered friends.

Yes, a wonderful, ragged scar.

Then I'll be more hideous than the ugliest of them. How envious they will be.

"Have some food," my first friend says. "These are great.

Real fresh."

She pushes a tray of Robert's toes and fingers under my nose.

And I choose the pinky because it still wears the ring I gave Robert for his birthday.

SOMEWHERE
IN THE NIGHT
Cruising with Andrew

I work the night shift. Full-time in winter, part-time in summer, I roam the floor of a noon-to-midnight boutique. Beyond the wide door and high windows, waves of the city's college students stream by. Their voices the rumble of distant surf, they flow from countless directions. High-tech fashion collides, merges, diverges, crashing over the street and sidewalk.

On occasion, a rivulet carves its way through the racks of clothes. I follow close behind, intoxicated by the warm scents. Filled with jealous hunger, I watch each one posture in our stylish apparel. I smile and nod, courteously answering queries about their fragile beauty.

This night, they are all beautiful. But the years will decay, even the fairest will wither and fade.

Perhaps some night far removed from tonight, one of them will have a twinge of recognition — "But no, you couldn't be him. That was *so* long ago" — through age-cracked lips. And

I, untouched by life's twisted consolation prize, will smile politely, unable to ease pain — theirs or mine.

"Andrew old boy, where you been hiding?"

Even tonight I am recognized.

An acquaintance from the former existence rummages through the shirts. "Haven't eyed you in class lately. The prof's been asking questions."

"Morning classes don't fit my — schedule — at the moment."

I sell the transient pretty boy a paisley shirt and striped tie, avoid further questions with flattery.

I'll see you around, too, Airhead.

Somewhere in the night.

O

The road of life is filled with sharp curves that conceal treacherous pits. Not so long ago, I stumbled into a crevice that cradled an ancient, dreadful entity. I now travel through that deep darkness, altered, enriched and deprived. I possess ageless knowledge, an endless future. I am spared the cruelties of time's ravages. But I miss showers and garlic bread and sunlit beaches; my tan is fading fast. Even in this age of all-night shopping, I cannot purchase a map back to the daylight. I can follow only the byways of the night.

O

Eleven forty-five. Another shift in the fashion industry drawing to a close. The flow of students is at an ebb — I can see the sidewalk again. Fifteen — no make that fourteen minutes — and the night is mine.

Then the stray wanders in.

From the cash register, the store manager glowers over the night's receipts.

Donning my most diplomatic smile, I descend on the night's last customer. "May I help you make a quick choice?"

His hand skims a stack of angora sweaters before he turns. Am I stunned or has the blood gone cold in my veins?

What word is more potent than beautiful—than gorgeous? What is beyond striking?

I stand a foot from him, yet his warmth scalds my skin. I try not to breathe, but his aroma reels my brain. Dumb, numb, I gape like the naive schoolboy I was not so long ago.

"Maybe a shirt," he replies. "And perhaps tie."

The years will decay — even the grandest beauty will wither.

But must it? I have escaped.

The manager bellows, "We close in ten minutes."

Ten minutes of unconquerable dilemma is more of an eternity than even I wish to face.

O

Chimes that only I can hear toll midnight.

While the manager prepares the night deposit, I loiter among the shirts and ties. The ringing in my head fades, my vision clears. My hand hovers over one, then another shirt touched by our last customer. Wisps of his warmth yet linger.

Beyond the high windows, only a few stragglers remain in the street. He is not among them, and I am glad. Momentarily, I have escaped the dilemma.

The manager hustles me into the street. The iron gate and glass door slide shut behind me. I cross against the light, hoping conscience will be more sensible and wait on the curb. No such luck. I relent to its companionship. Together we haunt the dark street.

Another essence tags along. I halt, glance around. I feel his warmth, taste his scent, yet see only pale, lifeless shadows.

The sensation persists.

I tremble with the knowledge that somewhere in the night he waits for me.

O

In a basement bar, I choose the night's mark. He is handsome, not compelling.

Yes! Compelling — the only word capable of describing the boutique's last customer.

My choice is handsome, but not so much so that the dilemma torments me. His face is not priceless — it is not compelling enough to be preserved for all eternity. He has had his time of beauty; I will spare him the anguish of the unrelenting decay.

I am still on my first drink as he finishes his fourth. We have spoken of inconsequential things. His words come slow and slurred. I glance at my watch, smile, suggest we get some fresh air. His bloodshot eyes widen with a liquid sheen; his handsome face beams. With a firm hand I steady him when he slips off the barstool. No scene, thank you. I prefer quiet exits. Reaching for my wallet, I suggest he wait outside while I take care of the bar tab. With the stalwart stiffness that only drunks can manage, he navigates his way to the door.

I wait. One — two — five minutes. I pay, leave a tip that will not be remembered as too cheap or too extravagant. Blind to the handsome faces that fill the bar, I leave, one face — a commonly handsome face at that — at the front of my mind.

The fingertips that slip inside my shirt are firebrands, white hot, against my stomach and chest; the tongue that flicks at the line of my jaw leaves a rivulet of molten rock that trails down my throat. He is too drunk to notice my arctic caress.

We are driven by the passions of alcohol and hunger. Wedged in a dark doorway on a deserted street, our embrace tenses; the courtship dance sweeps thought and emotion beyond our lurid surroundings. Yet, the crescendo cannot erupt here. I mutter the suggestion of discretion, of full realization and rapture to unheard music in a private, uninhibiting place. He presses his car keys into my trembling hand.

Shunning the idea of "my place or his," I steer his battered Toyota into the hills and a lonely precipice that overlooks ocean and city. Distanced from the risk of discovery — and from the turmoil of dilemma — I lead him to a bed of grass and leaves. The dance of rapture resumes, gains intensity, urgency. The heat of his body engulfs me. I take in each and every detail with each and every sense. We gasp and roll across the grass, release ourselves to the ultimate act.

At the height of the fever, I fumble for my jacket, search past the nubby material to the satin of the pocket. My fingers caress the onyx handle of my customized switchblade.

The dilemma is temporarily resolved.

O

By the time I return to my car, I have forgotten the commonly handsome face. Only the sensations of the encounter, the replenishment, remain with me as I walk, albeit unsteadily, through the parking structure. I am now the drunk with the stiff gait and purposeful movements.

My perception defies the haze of my stupor. Keys in hand, I falter beside my car. I am not alone in this deserted place. The scent that wafts above the odor of oil and exhaust is solid, touchable. My hand slips into the jacket pocket to keep my switchblade company. I turn in the direction of the aroma.

He stands in deep shadow, but shadows do not hinder my vision. The compelling face is unreadable. He still carries the plastic shopping bag from the boutique.

The dilemma swirls around him, a translucent specter forever on the prowl.

"I've been waiting for you," he says, walking toward me.

I resist the urge to follow the track of innuendo and keep my vision, blurry as it is, focused on his face. The big question: "Why?"

"You intrigue me," he replies with a flash of even white teeth. "You have for a long time."

A long time.... My mind repeats it again, once more, and jolts me.

"Really?" I sound weak, not at all intriguing. My thoughts are still hazed. I cannot concentrate while he is staring at me so curiously.

"My name is Brett," he says, stepping forward, hand extended.

I retreat and stumble, he catches me. His touch fires through my sleeve.

"I don't think you should drive," he says. "Allow me—"

"I'm fine." I pull free, firmly but not hard enough to reveal the extent of my strength. Still, the movement is too quick and throws me off balance. I fall to one knee, drop the car keys.

Brett is beside me in an instant. One arm across my back, he scoops up the keys before I can react. He helps me to my feet, guides me to the passenger door. His eyes never leave my face. "I'll drive you — wherever you want...."

Ohsurerightyeah. He'll drive me back to my apartment.

He'll help me inside. The living room's cool, but when he looks into the bedroom, gets a gander of the pewter-toned coffin where the king-size should be, he'll have questions to which I can give but one response. Death or death-life for the compelling Brett. The dilemma, straight and simple.

After we are settled in the car, me in the passenger seat, Brett behind the wheel, he places his hand on my leg. "I'll take you to my place. It's practically around the corner. You can rest, then drive yourself home when you're ready."

Reprieve.

Drunkenness, relief, and strange vestiges of fear collide in my brain. I collapse sideways across the seat, my head on his lap.

O

I retreat as far within myself as is possible without passing out. The drive to his apartment, how I got inside remain foggy black-and-white pictures. The only clear reality is the hours, minutes, and seconds until dawn.

My stupor breaks when his naked torch body stretches out against mine and his steamy breath sighs against my shoulder. My attitude remains unaltered, giving no hint of my awareness. I keep my eyes shut. I am not interested in the details of his room; I know his face completely — forever — even if I were never to look at it again.

The dilemma, naked and cold, stands at the bedside demanding comfort.

Do I kill Brett, taking every drop of his blood, leaving a decapitated shell as the final memory? Every encounter of my current existence has come to that verdict. Should this one be different or should I remain comfortably isolated?

Once or twice I have thought to leave the switchblade in

my jacket pocket in favor of the alternative. Each time I find myself filled with dread at the prospect. Without the switchblade there are responsibilities and obligations. Gotta find another coffin, gotta get it into the apartment, gotta get some dirt to line the bottom. My routine would become disrupted — straight home from work, no more wild, thoughtless flings.

Each time, I think about those restrictions, then I examine the face and wonder if it deserves ageless beauty. I ask myself if this person has any disgusting habits that might make me puke and — SNAP! out comes the switchblade, customized to Andrew specifications: eight-inch blade with razor-sharp edges for a nice clean cut. Sever the shackles of a three-thousand-or-so-year relationship before they can leave any bruises on my skin.

Weighing the other side of the scales' dilemma is the eternal "life" option. In Brett's case, the face, the body, perhaps even the person, deserve to be rescued from mortality's degradation.

I really don't have to take responsibility for him, do I? The considerate man who brought me to this state such a short time ago left me to my own devices. I was a whim — I was the beauty who should not whither. The consequences: weeks of confusion and anguish; catatonic despair. I was a wasted shadow before the insistent need forced me out into the night. I had no practical knowledge, skill, or prior experience. Only the need. After the first, messy encounter, I wished that Mister Considerate had been carrying a switchblade the night we met.

Can I be so cruel to Brett of the compelling face after he has been so kind to me?

Certain that Brett is sleeping, I slip from beneath his arm and out of bed. Step one toward the third possibility, a possibility that had not occurred to me before this moment. An alternative rising from the fullness of my veins from this night's earlier tryst.

I can just leave and allow Brett to live. No complications, no obligations, no intrusion into my existence.

I reach for my clothes.

"Where are you going?"

No simple escape.

"It's late. I'll be more comfortable at home."

"I'd hoped you'd be comfortable here," he says.

My back to him, I begin to dress. I am straightening the collar of my shirt when I realize I am standing in front of a mirror. Only Brett, head in shadow, shoulders and chest blue-hued in the moonlight, is reflected in the glass. I flick a hand at my hair, as if I can see it to straighten it, then sink into a chair to put on my shoes.

Fingers fumbling with the laces, I force myself to a decision. Alternative number three. After all, I do not need to kill him; I'm stuffed. Standing, I turn toward the bed yet look at the wall above it.

"Thanks for watching out for me," I say to a chrome-framed graphic. "But I'd better go."

"All right. Perhaps I'll see you tomorrow . . . . night."

He knows.

My hand slips automatically into my jacket pocket. All that torment over the dilemma when all along there has been but one answer. My fingers curl around the switchblade.

Stretching on the rumpled sheets, he smiles at my realization.

Unexpectedly, calm settles over me. He knows, but I do not feel threatened. His smile, his attitude toward me — what I am — is far different from anything I might have expected. I derive my existence from death, yet he is still attracted to me.

Then the chill strikes. I am frozen by a curve of his smile that I had not previously detected.

It is not *me* that attracts him but *what I am*. It is not *me* he wants to press his flame body against. He wants to have — to caress — to *be* the creature who survives on blood, who leaves innocents naked and decapitated on lonely cliffs. He would thrive on my existence. He would never suffer my dilemma.

I peer into the shadows in which he lies. I clearly see the compelling face, the sculptured body, and I am repulsed.

How many hearts and souls has he already devoured? How many innocents has he destroyed with that cold face and those stone muscles?

Naked enticement, Brett rises from the bed and walks toward me. "Did you decide to stay?" Eyes of pitch search my face; his hand explores my chest. "Andrew?"

Loathing — an emotion I have never felt toward myself — spreads through me. He is worse than I could ever be — more deplorable because he derives the pleasure of his existence from all pain — from all death.

A new dilemma rises before me — a ghastly, naked ghoul with Brett's compelling features. Do I destroy the monster now? Or do I let time wear at this human perfection until it is wrinkled, bent, and deformed?

The answer comes with a rising thirst. I have sated the need, yet it explodes again — demanding to be quenched.

With a quivering hand, I trace the lines of his brow, his cheek, his jaw — his throat.

No. Not with this blood.

From my jacket pocket, I extract the onyx-handled switch-blade.

The beast must not draw another breath.

The blade snaps open.

THIS APARTMENT POSSESSED

My car veers out of traffic and jolts to a halt curbside. Framed by the car window, a two-storied, two-winged apartment building stands back from the sidewalk. Maybe the original paint was turquoise; now it is faded lime. A metal sculpture, the iron highlighted by rust, hangs like a demented sun under the scrolled building numbers.

I shuffle through the shreds of Sunday's classifieds spread on the passenger seat. Broad red ink strokes smear the newsprint. Assigning the rejects to the floor, I select one small piece, nearly ripped in half, and re-read the brief description. Hardly exciting. I scrutinize the building. At least the walls aren't gang branded.

Upstairs, a one-bedroom apartment. Even with the windows open, I sniff faint mold. I explore the bedroom, bath, miniature replica of a kitchen. I loiter in the living room. My eyes slit, I picture my accumulated furniture — sofas, chairs,

tables, bookcases, plus a wall of stereo and TV accoutrement
— wedged into the room. My imagination leaves walking
space to spare. Circling, I pace out some haphazard dimen-
sions, to be on the safe side.

Dead halt. A faint outline on the green carpet. I crouch
down, trace the brownish stain. Dizziness; abstract images
behind the eyelids. I stand; the images fade.

I have forgotten the worst of them by the time I reach the
door.

On the landing, I relent to a nagging impulse. In the last
weeks, I've seen worse, but not better places. I search out the
manager. I itch to sign the lease.

O

Eight of us make an obnoxious moving crew. Laughing and
stumbling, we lumber up and down the metal and concrete
stairs, in and out of my new apartment from Friday afternoon
through the weekend. Boxes are dropped; heavy furniture
dragged across the floor. Eddie spends five hours assembling
the stereo, then cranks up the sounds. We lift as many beer
cans as boxes and carry in as many pizzas as furniture.

By Sunday evening, the old cracker box in the ghetto is as
empty and clean as eight drunk men can make it. The new
bread box apartment is loaded and ready to be trashed by the
celebration of our accomplishment. Three-day weekend; we
party as if isolated in the middle of an empty field.

The musty scent is replaced by fumes of liquor and sweat.
I open a window to let in fresh air and let out the ruckus. In
the courtyard, a young man — dark, wavy hair, good face,
even better body stuffed into tight t-shirt and shorts — glares
up at me. By the time I turn from the window, the notion of
hushing my boisterous friends loses importance. I accept

another beer, laugh uproariously when it foams down the front of my shirt.

O

Middle of the night. Shivering and disoriented. I roll over, bump into Eddie. For several seconds I do not recognize him; scares me. Even after I do, I am unnerved. Head pounding, I get up and pull on my jeans. I mistake the closet for the bathroom; I'm no longer in my old apartment.

Sprawled on his back, the sheets tangled around his ankles, Eddie snores lightly. Drapes billow, letting in the amber glow of flickering streetlights. In the far corner sits an extra chair that did not fit into the living room. I see a man sitting there. He stares back, eyes gleaming. I open my mouth — no scream. Force a hand toward Eddie. The movement alters the effect of shards of shadow and light that play across clothes piled on the chair.

My heart thumps; adrenaline courses through me. I tremble. Gasping, I stand lost, probably half-asleep. The digital clock on the night stand blinks away the minutes until I am able to move. Cautiously, I approach the chair, lift a shirt. Pesky illusion.

I back across the room to the bed, lie down, and pull up the sheet. I shed my jeans and slide across the mattress to the warm comfort of Eddie's skin against mine. I stare at the chair, afraid that if I shut my eyes the shadow man will be back when I open them.

O

During the next weeks, I take over my new place. Bits and pieces of myself are scattered around: worn toothbrush on the top of the toilet tank, half-read magazines open on the living room floor, underwear drying for days on doorknobs,

– 32 –

black-and-white prints of boffo men hanging on the walls. Home.

I empty the bedroom chair and make certain it stays empty. No more shadow men allowed.

I sleep with my face to the wall.

O

Nightmares start. Nothing substantial. Black and red slashed with streaks of silver. Grunts of agony reverberating.

O

I find myself, stark naked, pacing the length of the living room. Lights on; drapes open. On the television an ugly talkshow redneck attacks his guests while a brainless audience catcalls encouragement.

A late-night visitor knocks on my door.

"Who is it?"

"Zach. From downstairs," filters over the TV.

I open the door. Zach — dark, wavy hair, good face — gapes at my naked figure.

I am equally shocked. "Just a minute."

I shut the door in Zach's astonished face and run into the bedroom. Embarrassed, dumbfounded, then frightened. I glimpse the shadow man in my chair. Snatching up jeans and shirt, I retreat to the hall. While I dress, I am certain the shadow man watches.

Knocks on the door.

Memory of Zach worms back into my paralyzed mind. Buttoning my fly, I return to the living room. Extremely apologetic, I invite Zach inside.

Zach scrutinizes me severely before accepting my invitation. Scanning the living room, he hesitates. I follow his gaze, expecting to find that the shadow man has joined us.

"There've been some problems," Zach says. Nice voice, smooth and easy on the ear.

"Problems?"

"With the previous tenants." Zach glances at the TV. A commercial blares. He taps his watch. "It's late."

"Is it?" I have no idea what the time is. Zach's expression extorts guilt; I turn off the set.

"I don't want to be an old nanny," Zach says. His gaze glides over me; he tugs at the earring in his right ear. He seems to be having trouble maintaining his anger. "I'm up late most nights. But the TV and your prancing—"

"Prancing?" Interesting little word. I grin.

Zach struggles at seriousness. "Whatever you're doing comes through the ceiling pretty loud. I wanted to talk to you about it now. Nip it in the bud."

"Sit down. Can I offer you something?"

Shaking his head, Zach sits on the couch. "Late-night noise seems to be a problem with this apartment. The previous tenants — well, the later it got, the louder they got. Pacing from room to room. Playing the TV really loud."

"I'll try to behave," I promise him. "I'm sorry I disturbed you." Inspiration; I cross to the desk. "Let me give you my phone number." I scribble on a pad, extend the paper to him. I like the way his muscles stretch beneath his clothes as he stands and walks across the room. "If I forget, call me."

"Thanks . . . ." He glimpses the paper. "Mark." He smiles.

With a grin, I return the unspoken communication. Unfortunately, as Zach said, it is late.

He gives me his phone number — in case his digitally processed music soars too clearly through my floor — then he departs.

Leaning against the door, I listen for Zach sounds downstairs. I am rewarded with the muffled closing of a door, the whine of water through the wall pipes. Even when all is silent, I stare at the worn green carpet. Finally deciding to hit the hay, I discover that more than an hour has passed.

Two in the morning. Nothing more lonely. The old apartment building creaks; the streetlamp blinks off . . . . on . . . . off, creating shadow men in dark corners.

O

I see Zach occasionally — usually when I have Eddie or Lance or Tom in tow. Zach always smiles; I must be behaving.

I rarely see the shadow man in my chair. He has moved into my dreams. Every night.

O

My bedroom, the walls matte black. Fetid darkness that beads on the skin. Flashes of silver light that almost blind.

The shadow man's domain.

Hot breath at the back of my neck. A cool hand traces up my arm to my shoulder, around my throat, and cups under my chin. Disjointed words in a hoarse drone. My body shudders from the internals to the extremities.

He circles me. I learn his body by touch. His shoulder brushes mine: he is tall, for I am tall. Smooth chest and stomach; soft, untoned contours mold against me. His groin presses me with adequate strength. My fingers outline the planes of his face. The sharp bridge of the nose, the hollows of the eyes, the arch of the eyebrows. Fine hair fringes the high forehead. From his temples, I stroke the flat cheeks to the thin lips. My fingertips slip through something hot and wet on his broad chin.

Silver light strobes. Beneath a halo of dark blond hair, the face is erratically highlighted. Purple bruises mark the forehead; a long gash splits the brow. A network of broken veins bloats one eye; a smashed void gapes under the shriveled lids of the other. Black-red blood gushes over his bottom lips to splatter on my chest.

O

Awake. Choking on a scream. Flickering light burns my eyes; growling voices assault my ears.

Again in the living room, I wear a path in the thin carpet. On the television, the bigot hosts his rowdy talkshow. Panic. I hit the power button. I stand petrified, listening.

Nothing from Zach's apartment. The phone does not ring. Perhaps he is not at home to know that I have broken my word.

Exhausted from sleep, I sink onto the couch. I watch the blank TV screen. Around my haggard reflection, dull images cavort behind the glass.

I stretch out on the couch, turn my back to the television. Ragged breathing, jangled nerves. Dawn glows through the drapes before I find comfortable sleep.

O

A quiet evening. Book in hand, I sit on the couch. The stereo plays softly. I try very hard to behave.

The doorbell rings.

I snap the book shut, stare at the television. My mind drifts to worry that Zach has come for a confrontation.

Again the doorbell.

Setting the book on the coffee table, I cross to the door. Deep breath; I paint on an innocent smile, then pull the door open. Eddie stands outside. Relief brings a genuine grin.

"Eddie! Come in. It's been awhile." I think.

With stiff gait, he walks into the room. No pretenses with

Eddie. He stands silent and angry, nudging the coffee table with his knee.

"Something to drink?"

"Beer."

Good. Eddie has a firecracker temper, best taken with a strong dose of alcohol.

I break out the frosted mugs; Eddie is unmoved by the gesture. He takes a chair; I sit alone on the couch.

"We had a dinner date Saturday night," he says. The voice is on a tight rein. "I've been leaving messages."

Saturday night. How many days ago was that? Messages. On the table under the window, the answering machine rebukes me with its blinking red light.

"I must have forgotten," I sputter, and down half my beer. The rush of alcohol in the brain offers no protection.

"Forgotten?" His voice breaks with rage. He glares at me with those dark blue eyes. "Too busy tricking, wasn't that it, Mark?"

"Tricking?" I'm no fool; I gave that up.

"You were seen," Eddie snaps. "Tom couldn't believe his eyes."

"Where . . . ." I search my memory but cannot find Saturday night.

"At Lassoed. Hardly a sweater boy hangout."

Lassoed? Eddie's right; I never rode that range before.

"Maybe I don't have the right to an explanation." Eddie stands; the glasses on the coffee table rattle. "We're just friends. But you don't ditch your friends for a wild time in a back room."

Pieces start to come together. Mostly anatomy shots. A wide array of anatomy. I was very popular Saturday night.

"Mark?" Eddie storms toward the door. "Fuck it."

I want to stop him. I cannot move; words will not form. The door slams; I stare at it. My mind deserts my living room for a dim, smoky room and a dozen hunks in cowboy boots taking turns at me.

O

Full manifestation — and remembrance — of my nocturnal escapades.

In a sweat, I wake up. Barely breathing. The clock reads twelve-fifteen. Sweat freezing on my skin. Vestiges of another nightmare chafe my mind. A voice — the shadow man's? — drones close to my ear.

Hot shower. Cannot shake the chill. I dress, the works — slacks, shirt, sweater, socks, shoes. Back to bed.

Then, wind whipping through the open window, I wake up in my car. I drive without direction — yet I know where to make each turn, which street is the shortest route. I journey to neighborhoods dark and dangerous, neighborhoods where your car is stripped in five minutes, or your head bashed in, your wallet stolen, in one.

I enter establishments called Rough and Double-Jointed and Sleazy Pickings. Places that, until I pass under their neon signs, I did not know existed. Inside, men with faces carved of granite. Leather caps and vests or flannel shirts and jeans or cowboy hats and chaps. I stroll among them, impressed by the tight bodies. The patrons appreciate me as well. Hands explore me, guide me through to the bar. The smirking, occasionally winking bartenders set up drink after drink, paid for by this man or that. In my linen slacks and sweater, I am a fascination.

A back room. Pitch black. The musk of sweat and sex.

Rough carpet fibers dig through sweater and shirt to scratch the skin. Throaty groans. Dull thud of skin against skin. Intermingled ruggedness and tenderness; aloofness and intimacy. A chorus of ecstasy rings through the ears to the core of the body racked by total release.

Yet I remain detached from the experience. My body receives, my brain registers the pleasures. As if from across the room, I observe.

Then, a startling revelation in the midst of tangled, slick limbs. My self would not instigate such liaisons. Another step. My self does not control my actions. Sensations lightning through me. I squeeze my eyes shut but cannot extricate myself. My breath explodes in sobbed gasps; each nerve-ending fires with a shattering orgasm of lust and intellect.

The shadow man masters my being.

O

In panic, I escape. Men who bought me drinks try to detain me; they will be cheated by my departure. I break through barriers of groping hands and muscular bodies. On the street, I halt. A single streetlight burns; the sidewalk is deserted. I would be safer in the company of men, but I cannot endure further encounters. Physically or mentally.

The droning voice in my mind cannot dissuade me.

I walk half a block through wind-tossed darkness. A spotlight hits from behind; two separate, yet joined, shadows jump across the concrete from my feet. The roar of a motorcycle resounds through the street. Prickling fear at the back of my neck. The motorcycle idles up beside me. Dread expands. I sweat in the cool night. My eyes itch; my throat dries out. I walk faster; the motorcycle keeps pace.

The rider recites an invitation.

Full, uncontrollable terror. Ahead, I spot my car. I break into a mad dash. My footsteps rattle on the sidewalk. I fumble my keys out of my pocket. Skidding to a halt, I bump into the car fender, scrape my hip. Twist the key; jerk open the door. With a choked cry of success, I throw myself inside, lock the door. I suck down a breath, tremble as if I have just escaped the executioner.

The motorcycles edges past; the brake light flashes. My first glimpse of the rider: he wears a sports jacket and jeans; blond hair hangs in long strands past his shoulders. The engine whines, and the rider bolts up the street.

I grip the steering wheel, press my forehead against my hands. Laughter tumbles from deep inside. He was not the one.

O

Nightly ritual.

After dinner, I force myself to do the dishes. I creep from the kitchen to the living room. In silence, I settle in with a book and a beer. Twenty minutes later, and the words on the page swarm. I resist sleep until I am fully drunk. Around eleven, I tiptoe into the bedroom.

Bed. Never look at the chair in the corner; stare at the ceiling. I doze, but at eleven-fifteen I am standing in front of the bathroom mirror brushing my hair. I flee back to my bed, will myself to be strapped down by invisible chains. Eleven-thirty: the living room, TV blaring; I lift and drop furniture in search of my shoes. Retreat. Eleven-forty-five: bathroom again, rocking heel to toe on a creaking floorboard. Every fifteen minutes until my resistance crumbles and I dress for the road.

O

Middle of the night jog up the metal and concrete stairs. The apartment building quakes under my feet. Keys clank against the door as I unlock it. Leap inside, elbow the door shut. It crashes into the frame, jarring the windows. I stride into the kitchen, grab a beer, slam the refrigerator. Through the living room to the bathroom. Throw back the seat, let it fall shut. Living room. I hold a steady finger on the TV's volume control until the apartment swells with sound.

Flopped on the couch, I pour beer down my throat. The shoes pinch; the shirt confines. I toe the shoes off and kick them across the room. I peel my shirt open from sweaty chest and stomach.

From downstairs, I barely catch the sound of a door closing. The stairs creak. Footsteps hesitate outside my door. Three sharp raps.

Reluctantly, I tear my gaze from the television. I am not inclined to move.

The raps sound more insistent.

I thumb the TV remote. Beer bottle cradled in my arm, I saunter to the door and jerk it open. Tall, well-built cutie stands outside. My eyes travel down the folds of the t-shirt, hanging so enticingly from the muscles of his chest. I grin at the neat arrangement inside the running shorts. My hand tightens on the bottle. He clears his throat, and I drag my gaze to his face. Good face, even when blanched with anger.

"What is your problem?" he asks.

"Problem?" I swig at my beer. Recollection twitches in the brain. I know this one from somewhere. "There's no problem."

Total exasperation: "Then why are you storming around like fucking Godzillas on parade?"

I swing an arm around his shoulders. "Come in." I don't give him much choice, and shut the door. "We'll talk." I guide him to the couch. "Beer? Yeah, you need to chill out."

Maybe even put it in the freezer and save it for tomorrow. Utilize that energy for something other than an argument.

"We had an agreement," Zach says.

Yes, of course, Zach from downstairs.

"You were going to try to behave."

Like the perfect gentleman I'll behave.

I fetch fresh beers from the kitchen, then drop onto the couch beside Zach. I press my leg against his. Flashing my most winning smile, I offer him his drink. "Peace?"

"Not until we settle this." Yet, he accepts the beer.

"Obviously, I woke you." I do another, more detailed scan of him. "I am sorry."

"Obviously, you're not being sincere," Zach returns. "You're just as weird as the last three tenants. Quiet as the tomb all day. Lead boots and blaring TV after midnight."

"Very inconsiderate."

"You should know." He sets down the beer bottle. "You made a promise and broke it like the rest of them. Are you going to pack up and leave in the dead of night, too? Are you even listening to me?"

Like Eddie before him, Zach sees that the smug barrier which has overtaken me cannot be conquered. Zach seems frightened by what he sees on my face.

Pushing off the couch, he steps toward the door. "Maybe we can finish this later."

Unlike Eddie, Zach is not allowed to escape. I hook a finger into the waistband of his shorts. As I suspected; nothing in there but him.

"Don't be hasty," I say, standing. I slip one hand down the back of his shorts; the other hand finds its way up the front of his t-shirt. "Let's work this out."

"You're different . . . ."

How perceptive.

My hands maneuver; his resistance wavers. He tugs at my hair to unlock my lips from his throat. The sharp pains spur me on. I drag down the collar of his t-shirt, forge a trail down his chest with my tongue. I hit the perfect nerve; he is mine.

He skims my shirt off my shoulders. "Mark . . . ."

I chuckle. Mark's not at home.

O

As one being, we enjoy him. Double-image hands knead Zach's skin from the shoulders past the small of his back. In the mirror opposite the bed, two reflections hover over him. One is thin and dark: the substantial form that possesses this apartment. The other is heavier, blond: a translucent shadow that possesses the tenant. Their movements are not quite coordinated. The Mark stares curiously at the glass; the shadow man maintains the choreography of the sexual dance. Then the two figures unite to lead the unsuspecting Zach to spasms of rapture.

O

Over the next few nights, a dream recurs. Coiling fumes of oily leather. A whine that crescendos to a roaring scream. A slashing silver torch. Tumbling river of violence; waterfalls of blood. Black tar bubbles in an abyss of death. Progressive fragments layered one upon the other. At the apex, the shadow man, wearing my face as a mask, flounders.

O

Tonight, I have a mission — a quest — to fulfill.

Nervous cat on the prowl. I slink from one bar to the next. Do not stay long in one spot. If the face is not there, I return to the street. Even there, I study every man I encounter.

Cars slither up beside me; spiced suggestions waft from the open windows. I move on. Cars hold no interest. Motorcycles are more my speed.

Hours amble by; my determination tires. Fatigue gives the shadow man a stronger grip. He urges me to continue. *He is out there*, the hollow voice drones. *Patience; you will meet.*

Shortcut through an isolated parking lot. Perilous. Distant traffic sounds echo off crumbling brick buildings. Unsavory odors drift from scattered rubbish. Overhead, roaming clouds reflect the city lights, cast dusty illumination across fissured asphalt.

Under a dark streetlamp stands a motorcycle. A big, black bike of power. Scents of oil, exhaust, and leather cloud the air.

Inside me, the shadow man shivers with excitement.

From the shifting shadows, the man seems to materialize behind the chainlink fence. Tall; broad shoulders tapering to narrow waist. Cut-off sweatshirt reveals bulging biceps and heavily veined forearms. Twisting tattoos. Black boots scuff through the litter then scrape asphalt as he wedges through the broken fence. Fractured light gleams off the hollow face framed by dark, close-cropped hair. He sees me, halts. Thin lips twitch; a vile grin.

Only the motorcycle separates us.

"Alone?" he asks.

I nod; my voice might betray me.

He gestures at the heavy bushes beyond the fence.

Not here, warns the shadow man.

"We can do better." My voice sounds bold, bolstered by

the shadow man. I surrender to his will. No other way to survive.

The man straddles his motorcycle. His fist taps the seat behind him. "Hop on."

"My car's around the corner."

His eyes narrow. Then, a curt nod.

I lead the way. Just behind me, the growling motorcycle dogs my steps.

O

The single headlight beam bounces in the rearview mirror. My hands, palms sweaty, strain and flex around the steering wheel. In my head, the shadow man drones intricate instructions. A long time, he has waited; his patience is waning. My foot presses the accelerator down. In the rearview mirror, the headlight falls back, then, with a filtered roar, matches my speed.

I need a head start, if only a few seconds.

Park the car, race through the apartment building entrance. I leap onto the stairs; my footfalls rebound through the courtyard.

Zach at his window, staring up at me. He turns toward the entranceway; his face tightens.

The motorcyclist has arrived.

I burst into my apartment. A single lamp burns in the corner; too much light for the shadow man. I turn on the television; no sound. Turn off the lamp. Better. The flashing glow from the rapid TV images creates confusion for the eyes.

Bedroom. Root through the closet. My hand wraps around an aluminum shaft. I do not remember buying the weapon; the shadow man picked it out.

Noise in the living room. Thud of the closing door. Heavy footsteps, creaking floorboards. The motorcyclist is home.

My weapon concealed against my leg, I walk to the doorway. The motorcyclist paces a short path, his eyes transfixed by the television. He tugs on leather gloves. This time, he wields natural weapons.

"I've been here before," he says.

"I know."

"Someone else lived here."

"He still does." My voice sounds as two.

He smirks, unbelieving. He walks toward me. His leg bumps the coffee table, tips it over. He smooths the leather gloves over his knuckles, stretches his fingers, then coils his large hands to fists.

I hoist the baseball bat, revel in its weight and easy swing.

He hesitates, assesses me. The sharp features reflect confidence; he thinks me no match.

I strike. He deflects the blow with his forearm. Fury incited by pain, he snatches at the bat. I am too swift; I possess the agility of two men. I strike again, connect with the head. Blood drips from his ear.

Dazed but a moment, he lunges. He feigns a punch; I counter. His left fist slams against my cheek.

I crash against the wall. Cry of agony. Not from the blow. The shadow man tears himself free of me; pain sears like the flaying of skin. I falter, exposed, helpless. I look into the motorcyclist's face. Death's head.

His fist grinds my lips against my teeth. I choke on my own blood. His hand tangles in my hair. Jerked away from the wall. Flickering light blinds. My face smashes into hot glass. Dragged back, thrust into the TV screen again. Crackling: glass or bone?

He releases me; I crumble to the floor. Last strength. I hoist myself up, face my assailant.

Expression curious, he steps back. Diverted attention. The television fascinates him.

I crawl toward the door.

He watches the screen.

The vicious talkshow bigot hosts a rerun of murder. In lurid color; stereo where available.

The set is my apartment; different art director. The actors: the motorcyclist and the shadow man. The prop: an aluminum baseball bat.

Tight close-ups of hatred; of terror. Revealing longshots of brutality. The crime climaxes: crosscuts of the slashing bat and splashing blood.

The motorcyclist smiles at the final close-up of the victim.

The TV image fades. The screen remains black, leaving the room in dark shadows.

The shadow man returns. He folds his figure around me; a cocoon. He drags me to my feet and forces me toward his killer.

The motorcyclist snatches up the baseball bat. Spins toward us. He malice wavers. His attack is reflex.

We lift our hand; the aluminum stings like plastic. Effortlessly, we wrench the weapon from his grasp. The motorcyclist cowers before us. His hatred implodes to terror. We have recast him in the role of victim. We exact a much more satisfying denouement.

O

One by one, the senses register awareness. I feel throbbing pain. I taste blood, smell sweat. Frantic knocking at the door.

Opening my eyes, I see my reflection on the television screen.

I am a mess. Bruises on my face, torn skin, scratches of blood. I look enough like a victim to get away with murder.

I open my hand; the baseball bat clatters to the floor.

Voices of authority resound with the pounding. Limping, I cross to the door. Two policemen, Zach behind them, stand on the landing. They gape at me, then at the body on the floor in front of the television.

"He followed me," I stammer. "Tried to kill me. I think he's dead."

The policemen prod the motorcyclist, examine the bloodied baseball bat. They turn to me in wonder.

Zach helps me to the couch. I settle back, then look again at the television.

An after-image of the shadow man fades from the screen.

CHARACTER DEVELOPMENT

*E*very morning for the last three weeks — at precisely 8:00 a.m. — Edwin Spurlock would station himself at his desk and poise his fingers over the typewriter keyboard. Every morning — at precisely 11:00 a.m. — Edwin would retreat to his bedroom for a long nap. For the last three weeks, the paper in the platen, equally determined, had remained blank.

Edwin's naps were not entirely without use. In his procrastinator's delirium, Edwin dreamed of people he did not know, people who inhabited the world that Edwin wanted to create. They walked and talked and enacted their dramas on a well-rounded tableau. They had backgrounds and futures, hobbies and jobs, specific shades of the spectrum of hair color and the minutest detailing to their garments. But, in that brief moment between sleep and consciousness, in that fragment of groggy time before Edwin forced his eyes to open, all the people with their intricate lives would flee into clouds of blue-gray. Edwin would rise from his nap, more exhausted than when he lay down, and know that the multitudes had been with him and that he had somehow frightened them off.

After naptime, Edwin dutifully returned to his desk. Still half-asleep, he regarded the typewriter as some abhorrent metallic science-fiction monster and confined it to a far corner. From the other corner, he dragged a spiral notebook, opened it, and faced a page that was not quite as blank as the one in the typewriter. Some paper company in the Midwest had been thoughtful enough to print blue lines on this page; it seemed less daunting.

Positioning the notebook at the perfect angle, Edwin scratched out a few words: the day and date. With a plaintive sigh, he sat back in his chair, chewed at the end of his pen, and thought. But the blue-gray clouds in his mind guarded their secrets well.

Before long, Edwin's eyes became heavy and the pen drooped in his hand. He leaned closer and closer to the spiral notebook. At first his head was supported by his left hand; then he sank farther, resting his head on his arm, allowing the pen to fall to the nearly blank page. A drop of ink spread a spidery lace across the paper.

O

"I believe he works too hard," announced the old lady with the grizzled white hair, over-sized handbag, and flannel stockings. "He reminds me of my late husband, Alexander. Now, Alexander was a worker. Day and night. Night and day."

"Everyone knows all we need to know and more about Alexander," said the thirtyish man decked out in tight blue jeans, open-necked Oxford cloth shirt, and suede boots. He pulled at a pitch-black sideburn. "I think our man is just fucking burnt out. No one can sit down every day, accomplish nothing, and not become just fucking burnt out."

"Don't swear at Grammere. It burns her ears like lava would burn your hands." The gangly teenager tore off his rimless glasses and frantically cleaned them with the tail of his soiled t-shirt. "Grammere never swore once in her entire life." He gave the glasses a little shove up onto his nose and glared at the man. "Grammere hates *that* word."

"'S'all right, boy," the old lady said, hobbling to the desk and looking over the sleeping man's shoulder at the scrawled words. She shook her head, adjusted a handmade shawl with an arthritic hand. "He works too hard. Much too hard."

O

Edwin shot up from the desk and out of his chair. The afternoon sun slanted through the windows, filling the room with a faint pink glow. Rubbing his neck, Edwin crept around the room, looking in the odd place — inside the bookshelves and behind the file cabinet — for he-was-not-sure-what. He paused at the table before the window, his hand poised over the yellowed doily, and sniffed the air. There was a scent, like lavender, lingering, and something more pungent, like oil. He peeked under the doily before returning to the desk.

The page was still blank save for the printed blue lines and the day and date. With a defeated grimace, Edwin returned the spiral notebook to its place, repositioned the typewriter for tomorrow. He filled the evening hours with the flickering box in the bedroom.

O

Tomorrow progressed the same as yesterday. Edwin was

right on schedule. Typewriter; nap; spiral notebook; nap. The ink from his pen splattered strands of his blond hair.

O

"He is too young and handsome to pass his days so miserably," the auburn-haired woman with the faint silver eyeshadow whispered. With a delicate hand, she skimmed the smooth cheek of her own face. "One so young and handsome should be enjoying life, but our poor boy . . . ." She tisked her way around the desk, her sheer chiffon sleeve trailing over the sleeping man's hair.

"Handsome be damned," said the man in the tight blue jeans. He traced a jagged line from his eyebrow to his jaw. "See this scar? This is what handsome gets you. Bar brawl — nineteen eighty-three — switchblade wielded by the ugliest motherfucker you ever—"

"Grammere hates that word!" the teenage boy shrieked. "She fucking hates it . . . ."

The man tugged at his pitch-black sideburn and guffawed. The chiffon-draped woman pressed her long, slender fingers to her ample bosom. The old lady's wide nostrils splayed with greater disapproval.

O

At his usual time, Edwin shut his book and set it in its impression in the nightstand's dust. He dug through the bedclothes for the remote control and beamed off the television across the room. Eyes straying to the door — beyond which was the living room, the desk, the waiting typewriter, and the spiral notebook — Edwin turned off the lamp and slipped under the covers.

Patiently, he stared at the ceiling above, waiting for his upstairs neighbor's nightly ritual of squeaking floorboards, thudding shoes, and running water to reach its conclusion. *Crash* . . . . *crash* . . . . *creak* . . . . *creak* . . . . and the behemoth was settled for the night. Quiet surrounded Edwin, and he shut his eyes to dreams of that blue-gray-cloud world.

Some few hours before dawn, that elusive realm opened before him, a swirl of haze and muted light. Yet something was different. Had he been deserted or were the inhabitants merely on vacation? His dream-self searched high and low, near and very far, but none of the people with the perfect shades of hair and detailed clothing could be found.

His dream-self blinked and was returned to his bed. He lay there, unnerved, immobile, knowing that something was near, waiting in the undulating clouds. There came a sigh, low and weary — a shuffle of movement, edging closer. His dream-self tensed.

The apparition appeared without warning at the foot of the bed. In the first moment, it was but a tall shape, vaguely reminiscent of a human being. Then, by flashing degrees, the shape altered, defining itself in head, torso, arms, and legs. One moment it was bald; the next, long hair stirred around the void of its face. The torso was flat and sexless. A lacing of mist, a shimmer of light. The shoulders widened, the chest expanded, the stomach flattened, and the sex was enticingly pronounced. Large hands flexed; biceps bulged. Sleek muscular legs shifted on high-arched, slender feet.

Edwin's dream-self surveyed the prime male figure as it rounded the bed. The dream-self shivered when he saw the face, as of yet bearing only traces of full lips, thin nose, high cheekbones — and eyes. Something was peculiar about those slightly slanted eyes.

Long hair shadowing the face, the man bent over the bed.

A large hand reached out and drew back the bedclothes. The perfect body molded against Edwin's dream-self. He gasped at the words that reverberated in his ears before the man melted into him.

O

On the first day of his fifth week, Edwin decided on a new tactic — lists, charts, and graphs. With a fresh carafe of coffee at one elbow and a fresh carton of cigarettes at the other, he opened a virgin notebook to the first blue-lined page. Bolstered by the dawn of the day and the week — why, yes, Edwin thought, even of life! — he ceremoniously inscribed day, date, and time at the top of the page. Without hesitation, he circled a "1" and boldly printed the first name from the list of characters which was stapled to the drapes.

Through careful research, cross-checking, and double-verification of his new methods, he began to create a living entity — a birth, a childhood — adolescent, adult. And he continued; yes, continued into, then completely through his 11:00 a.m. nap. The living entity swelled with a memory, with hopes for a future, and with the filmiest foreshadowing of death. Into the afternoon, beyond the amber glow of sunset, Edwin glided pen from page to page, incident to incident toward the realization that had eluded him so long.

Then, some minutes before the broadcast of the final round between two squealing housewives for a brand-new, fuel-efficient car, Edwin Spurlock hesitated. But for a moment. The hesitation extended to a pause; the pause to a gaze-wandering distraction. The ink retreated into Edwin's pen, and the point dried out.

O

The auburn-haired woman tapped a fingernail against the

slightly chipped incisor of her otherwise perfect teeth. Never in her six months, two weeks, and four days as receptionist for the law firm on the upper southside had she witnessed such a tragedy. She shook her head in that way she had — once to the left and twice to the right — and uttered a high-scaled sigh. "The young should not face such turmoil."

"My Alexander experienced many a moment of dread and discomfort in his day," the old lady stated, bending low to tug at a fallen flannel stocking.

"No doubt," agreed the thirtyish man. He flashed a grin that accentuated his scar. "Living with a chatterbox bitch like you."

The gangly youth yanked off his glasses, made as if to toss them to the ground, then, after a thought, handed them to the ample-bosomed woman. Hiking up his stained jeans, he advanced toward the man with the pitch-black hair.

"You are all such fools."

The quiet voice held reign in the hazy realm. The four paused, each searching expansive memory for recognition of the voice, but not one of them found a link to occurrences past. The voice belonged to a stranger.

"There is no tragedy," the voice informed them. "And — as of yet — no motive for quarrel or physical violence."

The stranger materialized from the blue-gray clouds to confront them face-to-face. He was tall — over six feet — with sunstreaked hair and a suede jacket that had experienced a life of difficult struggle. The stranger's smile was friendly, but lacked sincerity's warmth. And his eyes — one was Caribbean-Sea blue, the other Sahara-Desert white.

"Who are you?" The old lady clutched her over-sized handbag.

"You will know me — quite well — soon enough," he replied. He ambled to the sofa where the sleeping man was stretched. "You must have patience with our Mister Spurlock. He has had a busy day and is tired." Absently, he pulled the blanket up to the sleeping man's chin, smoothed stray hair from his cheek. "At the proper time, he will be ready for each of you."

"The bastard will never be ready, not with those flow charts and color-coded traits—"

The stranger turned to them; his grin curled in a challenge. "Devices in a moment of uncertainty. Means to an end." He walked into their midst, bringing a fragrance of wind and earth. "The road to a breakthrough." A strong hand, the fingernails neatly clipped, swung toward the desk, spread with the map of intersected lives, the lists of virtues and vices, and the notebook open to a nearly filled page. "That — my friends — is me." The eyes of different shades turned in the tanned face to touch each of them.

The old lady clenched her handmade shawl. The black-haired man rubbed nervously at the hip of his jeans. The gangly teenager cleaned his glasses and secured them to his nose. The woman smoothed her blouse and revealed her chipped tooth in a coy smile.

"The crux of it, my friends," said the stranger, "is that none of you can live without me." From a pocket of his suede jacket he extracted a pipe; he struck a match with his thumbnail, sucked in the yellow flame. "And without me . . . ." in an odorous cloud of smoke ". . . . none of you can die."

O

To the right of the typewriter lay the notebook with its two hundred pages of tight script, to the left a thick stack of typewritten sheets. Edwin Spurlock picked up the last piece of blank bond. In his mind thundered a shotgun blast. A shrill scream rang counterpoint. Edwin's fingers tapped swiftly over the typewriter keys, and the last ink of the ribbon impressed "The End" to five complex, tri-dimensional lives.

THE DARK RED DAY

When the nightwind comes up chill and wet
And the sky burns eternal red,
A dirge shall moan for the unpaid debt
And the earth unleash the angry dead.

Dust from the road feels gritty in my teeth, the smell of the day pungent in my nostrils as I drive into town. With the convertible top down, the sun, hanging in a whitish-blue sky, burns my scalp and glares off the car hood through my sunglasses. The yelp of a dog that is to be someone's dinner rings in my ears.

My home town is one of those dirt-poor towns found anywhere in the country. Turn off any million-dollar highway onto a back road, and one of those towns awaits. Colorless clapboard houses, a general store that has not had decent stock in years, maybe a diner that serves mystery-meat as the luncheon special — that is the kind of town in which I was born and bred. A dirt-poor town occupied by dirt-poor people.

I escaped years ago. Unsatiated passion, held in suspension for more than a decade, brings me back.

I pull the convertible into the Texaco station with the

rusted, 25-year-old pumps. I went to school with the shaggy man who comes out to fill my tank.

"Hello, Carl," I say, climbing out of my car. "It's been a long time."

"Richard," he replies as if we spoke only yesterday. Carl is not as interested in me as in my car; three years old, I bought it used. Carl reacts as if it is a Rolls.

I look around the station. The newest vehicle on the lot is an early sixties pickup that Carl drove our last year of high school. From the office, dark faces peer through smudged, discolored glass. I smile, nod. The faces ignore me; they are as entranced by the car as Carl.

"Check the oil?" he asks in his most dry, disinterested gas jockey baritone.

"It was just changed."

Carl's red-rimmed eyes focus on me. They flash from my newly styled hair to the whiteness of my running shoes, not missing a detail of my linen shirt or stone-washed jeans. Those eyes burn holes through my wallet as I shuffle through the greenbacks for a twenty.

"Everyone still around?" I ask, handing Carl the money.

"Where would they go?" Carl skulks into the office for my change. Low voices greet him; he grumbles his reply and shoots a glance at me. I take a step back, bump into the car fender. I steel myself against uncertainty as Carl walks back. With hot eyes and cold expression, he drops the change into my hand.

"Thanks, Carl."

He stands rigidly, grease-stained hands twitching. Shoving the money into my jeans pocket, I fumble with the door handle, jump into the car, and make a hasty retreat. I draw in a breath to settle anxiety and confusion. In the rearview mirror, Carl, a gray figure against the gray gravel, stares after me.

O

The road through town snakes off in narrow side streets that dead-end at the woods. Tall trees oblivious to poverty shadow the town with luxuriant foliage. Through that obscurity, I see the town watching me.

Touchstones of memory impede my progress. I cannot resist visiting the haunts of my youth: the general store, the barber shop, the school. Old Man Wilson treats me with grim politeness when I pay for a pack of cigarettes with a ten-dollar bill. Joseph Turner mutters how nowadays a man, whether he has the two bucks or not, does not get his hair cut every two weeks — all the while staring, no doubt suspecting that my haircut is not a two-dollar job. Feigning interest in her recess charges, Mrs. Fletcher purses cracked lips at the news that her one-time favorite sixth-grade student managed a scholarship to a respected university.

I walk away from each of them feeling as if my jeans have shrunk around my groin. My abdomen tightens with uneasiness and forces a sour taste into my mouth. I cannot fathom why each of them, expressions shifting, looks at me from the corners of his eyes. They all knew me as a child; they seemed to accept me then. Could a dozen years make that much difference?

I am over-reacting, I tell myself. I imagine their hostility. But an after-image of Carl seems painted in thin watercolors on the rearview mirror.

O

Afternoon has set in by the time I reach my destination.

Clouds scud in front of the sun, tossing a shadow over the house. I have not been to this house since the night I ran away, yet a faded memory of it is always with me. More than once I have dreamed that I returned to it and to the person who lives within its dingy walls. Some of those dreams have realized all my hopes; some have not. Alone in the abandoned section of town, I am taunted by the unhappy endings which always left me gasping and dripping sweat in the cold hours of the night.

Sometimes when you are seventeen and you have known no other town than one like this town, confused emotions swamp you. A tiny voice warns you to keep your mouth shut. You are certain that you exist alone; everyone you know disappears. Then, out of the pitch of night comes someone who just might share the secret. You dance around the secret, perform the duties of life, and wonder if maybe, just maybe. . . .

Prying my hands off the paintless fence, I walk to the torn screen door. The secret was never shared, not even on the night I ran away. Apprehension chokes me. The secret should have been revealed — a promise made.

Life holds no certainties, but I need some guarantee that knocking on this door is not a mistake.

I cannot retreat. Even if I made no promise to him, I made one to myself.

The hinges shriek when I pull the screen door open. A breeze twists across the yard, rattling the insect-ridden bushes against the fence. A rat scratches its way from beneath the porch and scuttles across the dead grass to the woods. I knock — the sound reverberates inside; the wood stings my knuckles.

The impulse to run back to the car shudders through me. I force the urge down, wait, and knock again. The shadows around me deepen. In the sky, frail clouds stretch in all directions, blotting out the blue.

When I turn back, the door is opening. My fingers itch for a cigarette. His face pallid from sleep, James stands within reach again. His black hair is disarrayed around a face prematurely etched with age. He wears only a pair of wrinkled, faded red gym shorts. His green eyes flick over me, then lock on my face. The vestiges of sleep clouding his face vanish, a moment of shock, disbelief, and finally, a smile.

"Richard." He says it so simply, so matter-of-factly. My apprehension falls away like unwanted clothes.

"Jamie." Nervousness returns when he looks beyond me to the convertible outside the fence. "Too early for an old friend to get a cold beer?" I ask, resurrecting a ritual from the past.

James's smile brightens; he remembers. I let my defenses down. He steps aside, motioning me forward. "The bar is always stocked." He really remembers.

Following him to the kitchen, I steal glances into the living room, the downstairs bedroom. The furniture is the same, more worn. The overstuffed chair still sits opposite the bed. In a hazy flash of reminiscence I see two teenage boys in the bedroom. One dark, stretched out on the bed; one blond, curled up in the chair, they are laughing.

A half-full case of longnecks sits pushed against the wall; I do not feel so guilty about not bringing anything. James takes two bottles out of the refrigerator, opens them, and gives me first choice. I take the one in his left hand. Another old sacrament.

I am disappointed when James walks past the bedroom toward the living room. I want to sit in that chair again. But there is no need to barricade ourselves in his bedroom. Since his parents' deaths, James has had the house to himself.

The lamps James methodically circles the room to turn on cannot wash the gray from the frayed lace doilies on the end tables or the yellow from the lampshades. Uncomfortable, I sit on the couch. James wedges himself into the cracked vinyl recliner. Ashes fill the chipped ashtray on the coffee table between us. I reach for my cigarettes; James pulls a fresh pack of Pall Malls from the drawer of the table beside him. We stare at each other, sipping beer, exhaling thin streams of smoke.

"Have you seen Alex yet?" James asks to break the familiar silence — the silence where, to my thinking, each of us contemplates the secret.

My brother is my last concern. Ten years apart, we never had much use for each other. I only hear from Alex when someone in town dies. "I might stop later."

The silence again, accompanied by mutual assessment. How long will we sit and stare at each other before the wall of years crumbles and we can talk easily? I seek questions or comments, but they all sound stale. I do not want to waste time discussing the weather, jobs, or the state of the union. I light another cigarette as if its smoke will infuse me with the courage to tell James why I am here, to tell him that I do not want to drive back to the city alone.

"I thought I would take you to dinner," I manage.

He looks skeptical, grins. "At the diner?"

"They must serve something edible."

James laughs, a clear, free sound these surroundings have not darkened. He stands, nonchalantly tugging at the legs of his gym shorts. "If you're going to wine and dine me at the finest place in town, I should shower and change."

Our next moves could not have been orchestrated more precisely; there is a certain perfection in chance. He leans down to pick up his beer bottle from the coffee table; I lean forward to stub my cigarette in the ashtray. Our faces come within inches; our eyes touch.

In that second, the secret crackles like a fragile thread of lightning between us.

"Perhaps dinner could wait," I say.

James straightens; I stand. Our hands rise from our sides and intertwine. His palms are rough, calloused. We each round the coffee table in a step. After years of waiting, I trace my hand up his side and around his back; his arms circle me, his face presses against my neck. We cling to each other as if to meld into one person.

O

The years of fantasizing about our time together did not breed expectations beyond the limits of reality. But the details of the experience belong to me; I will not share them.

Afterward, we lie close in the darkness of his room. Wind seeps around the edges of the window sash, brushing our sweated skin. In that quiet time, I whisper plans that I made before I left the city. Trepidation returns; I tremble. James makes no comment; he stares at the shadows laced across the ceiling.

"I've done too much," I say. "I've plotted your future the same way I traced my route here on a map."

I try to separate myself from him. His fingers move lightly through the hair of my chest; his whiskers scratch against my shoulder.

"I don't resent that," James whispers, but his voice is guarded. "This town has been cruel to me — to anyone who has ever lived here."

He lifts his head and looks at me. Through the shadows, his eyes glisten sadness. "I just never thought I would have anything else. When you left, I wanted to climb out that window and go with you. But — even here — there's security. I might be hungry at times, but I won't starve. I might be cold, but I'm sheltered. It's safe here. I'm not as brave as you."

"I'm not brave, Jamie. I ran away. I left you because I was too frightened to ask you to come with me. I was afraid to tell you how I felt."

He nestles against me, smooth and warm. "We were both afraid of that. I think I still am. They knew about us then. They'll know why you've come back."

I glance at the window. Was that fleeting silhouette against the glass a swaying bush or a retreating man? I hold James closer, try to say that things will be different in the city. Words will not come; sometimes, the city is no different at all.

O

The smell of old grease and burnt coffee permeate the diner. The nicotine-stained fluorescent lights cast an unnatural hue to the faces that greet James and me when we enter. I know all the faces, although most are grayer and more creased, and all the faces know me. Recognition is inescapable, but it is the other emotion on those faces that disturbs me. Being with James again, still comfortable from our reunion, I ignore my forebodings. Tomorrow those faces and their rigid expressions will be relegated to the past.

We sit in an orange plastic booth, and Agnes, whose German ancestors were foolhardy enough to settle here, drops two plastic glasses of water on the crumb-littered table. Vacant black eyes pierce me while she drones the dinner specials. James barely shakes his head at the mention of the meatloaf, and I finally remember the truth the yelp of the dog represents. To the roast chicken, James nods and sips from his water.

"Two beers and the chicken," I tell her.

Frowning, Agnes waddles away.

"What's with her?" I ask James. "The chicken really her pet parrot?"

Quiet — total and complete. James sets down his water, shifts in the booth. I glance around. The other customers have turned, eyes slitted, lips twisted. Agnes stands in front of the kitchen door, her hand clawed around her pencil.

"It was just a joke."

She thrusts through the kitchen door; it swings back and forth behind her, unleashing a violent clash of pots and pans and bursts of heated air.

O

James and I have just started eating when a hulking shadow stretches across the food, and a voice I know too well bellows: "I heard you were in town." My brother Alex, all beergut and stringy blond hair, towers over the booth, his pale eyes all but hidden by bushy brows, his bloated lips contorted in what he undoubtedly considers a welcoming grin.

Without invitation, Alex plops into the booth beside James, scans our meal ravenously, then levels those nearly obscured eyes on me. Like everyone else in town, he takes in every detail, going so far as to lean over the table to examine my running shoes.

"Carl's been tellin' everyone 'bout that car of yours," Alex says, picking up my beer mug. He drains it in a swallow. "Agnes, another round!" — without taking his gaze from me. "What's it like, drivin' a car like that one? Feel good?"

"It's just a car, Alex. I got it used from a friend."

The grin curves oddly; he nudges James. "Used. Hear that, Jamie? Bet them clothes is used too."

Slopping beer, Agnes sets three mugs onto the table. "You eating or just drinking, Alexander?" she coos, pencil and pad poised.

Something shines in his eyes; he settles back in his seat. "I think I'm eatin', Agnes. Think my baby brother wants to buy me dinner. Right, baby brother?" He scans her from head to foot, licks his lips. "I'll have the meatloaf. Lots of gravy." He winks; Agnes pirouettes and returns to the kitchen.

Reaching across James's plate for the salt, Alex drags his sleeve through the gravy. He tips the salt shaker over his beer mug, sees the gravy, and sucks it out of his cuff. James drops his fork into the middle of his food and shoves his plate away.

"You don't mind buyin' my dinner, do you, Rich?" Alex asks. His gaze drifts to James's abandoned plate. "Specially since you didn't drop in on me and the family." Absently, he picks up James's fork and tears off a piece of chicken. "Can you believe that, Jamie? Been in town all day and hasn't stopped in on the family." Chewing, he leers at James. "Why do you suppose that is?"

"The multiple reasons elude me," James replies calmly, but he takes a long swallow from his beer.

Alex squints his uncertainty, then grabs the plate of meatloaf out of Agnes's hand. "More beer, Agnes." For an instant, he contemplates both the meatloaf and the chicken, and I see visions of him combining the two into a culinary delight. Surprisingly, he settles for the meatloaf.

"I have my own theories," Alex says, spewing a chunk of meatloaf.

I remember that James said the town would know why I came back. With my fork, I twirl a crater into my mashed potatoes; James waits expectantly for my elder brother's insight. For the moment, Alex seems content with his meatloaf and our discomfort.

After a slug of beer, Alex states: "I think Rich has been too busy drivin' that fancy *used* car around for everyone in town to see." The bushy eyebrows sink low; the shadowed eyes beneath shift between James and me. "I think he's been too busy flashing ten and twenty spots at the fillin' station and general store to stop in and pay his respects to his family." He scrutinizes each of us once more. "Course it's just a theory of mine."

If the town has always known the secret, if the town knows why I have returned, was Alex's "theory" an analogy — or was I considered guilty of another crime?

Everyone in the diner is glaring at me. How simple the answer. They disapprove of my pursuit of James, and they think I am flaunting my car and flashing around my money. The reactions of everyone I encounter come back like restless banshees. This is a dirt-poor town with dirt-poor people, and I cruise in behind the wheel of my convertible as if I wanted them all to know that I owned the outside world. The faces in the diner not only loathe my corruption of James, but despise my fortune and wealth-drenched pride.

"Are Charlene and the children home now?" I ask.

"Uh-hmm," around a mouthful of meatloaf. "Watchin' the

TV." Alex gives me a gravy grin. "Same old TV we had when you lived here."

"Agnes, the check," I call, reaching for my wallet. Every person in the dinner gapes when I open it; I wonder how far Carl exaggerated my petty cash. "We'll just go over now and see them."

I glance at James; he looks confused. He is one of them, allowed to share their ground as long as he is unobtrusive. He is too much one of them to see the threat in their pale faces.

"Should I call Charlene first?"

Alex shakes his head, watches as I select enough money to cover the bill and tip. He grins again when I stand and shove the wallet back into my pocket.

"Alex, I hate to interrupt your feast," James, trapped in the booth, says.

Shoving another bite into his mouth, Alex stands and lets James out.

"See you at the house," I say to my brother. I nudge James through the gauntlet of townspeople toward the door.

O

Clouds clog the sky; a damp wind scrapes my face as James and I walk across the parking lot. I feel nauseous, but not from the chicken. The anxiety spreads when I see Carl and two other men standing by the convertible.

"Are you all right?" James asks, touching my arm. "Why on earth did you say we were going to see Charlene?"

"We're not." My voice will not rise above a whisper.

He places a hand on my shoulder. We are standing too close, too intimately while under the watchful eyes of Carl and his two friends.

"We're going back to your house. We'll pack whatever you want to take. We're getting the hell out of here."

I look at him for the first time since we left the diner. James hesitates, obviously shocked by the expression on my face. He clamps his hand around my arm.

"Richard, we grew up with these people. We've known them—" He jerks his head toward the car.

Carl and his two friends are walking in some strange slow motion across the lot. From behind us comes the slam of the diner's door. They have all come out, headed by Agnes with her pencil and pad and Alex with his beer mug. Unhurriedly, they advance. The gravel under their feet explodes like twenty-five-cent firecrackers.

James presses against my side, his face reflecting the fear that has overtaken me. My hand finds his arm, and I guide him toward the less formidable obstacle: Carl and his two friends. My other hand fumbles in my jeans pocket for the car keys. My wallet feels like a concrete block in my back pocket. I wonder if throwing the money and credit cards to the mob would do any good.

White shapes and kaleidoscopic color edge through the darkness across the street. More people — children to senior citizens — descend toward the convertible. Mrs. Fletcher, long gray hair and striped pastel dressing gown whipping around her, leads the pack. Carl and his two friends stop to wait for her.

The town surrounds us. Silent, they close in. Their faces are blank, waxen in the dim nightlight; their eyes are voids. The group circles as if guided by collective thought.

I force myself to speak in an even, clear voice. "What do you people—"

"Richard, it's useless," James says.

"It's not useless." I am feeling galvanized, superior to these people. "We've never done anything to you. We've stayed out of your way. We have every right to our lives. Alex—"

Alex drops his beer mug. His hands stretch toward us. The others tread over the mug; the glass cracks, shatters under their weight. Another hand reaches out; another, fingers groping.

It is useless to argue with their ignorance — with their jealousy.

Bony fingers clutch at my sleeve; Mrs. Fletcher, expressionless, stands at my side. A cry from James. Agnes fumbles at his thrashing arms; Old Man Wilson snags James's shirt and jerks him away. He disappears in a whirlwind of hands and arms, is dragged into the tightening circle of townspeople. He shouts my name; the sound is cut off.

I stand alone in the center of them; they pull me in every direction. For the moment, they seem intent on watching my dread escalate. A finger pokes me, retreats, another from a different angle. I turn to Alex. One glimpse tells me that he — all of them — are beyond reason. The eyes beneath the bushy brows glow with malice; the bloated lips twist in glee.

Someone kicks me in the back. Carl draws back a foot and strikes with his steel-toed boots. I stumble. Joseph Turner kicks my arm. I lose my balance. I grab at Alex, but he shrugs me off, and I fall to one knee. Flailing boots and shoes overwhelm my vision. I recoil, try to crawl away. They kick me again . . . . again . . . .

Ghastly faces hover above me, a swirling montage of features. Pain explodes in my back, my sides, my groin.

Gravel bites into my face, the stale taste of stone in my mouth, the sour smell of dirt. I hear something snap; a bolt of agony fires up my left arm to my shoulder. I lift my head, blinking away tears. A hazy figure looms before me, then comes to crystal focus. My nephew, six years old, features cold rock, swings a foot. My faces goes numb except for a lava flow down my cheek.

Wet pitch envelops me. The pain recedes. I can still hear them kicking me. Distant, an echoing wail from a nightmare, I hear James screaming my name.

O

I cannot see; I cannot feel anything; I cannot think. Yet my hearing — filtered, distorted — remains intact. Muffled voices surround me.

"I'm next of kin!" Alex's voice. "It's mine, damn you all. The car, wallet — everythin' is mine."

A hissing whimper — the wind; crackling — leaves under feet; gurgling — the river: these sounds, fractured and reverberating, register, identified by instinct more than reason.

"Pretty Jamie won't say nothin' if we keep him busy." Alex's voice again. "I got *big* plans for him."

Then limbo. Brief rush of air past my ears. Sinking into cold damp; back in the womb, floating helplessly. Suspension in nothingness.

O

I am hanging by my hand. A chill wind spirals around me. I force my eye to open. The ground floats past, shiny; I am half-buried. I try to move; the earth is insubstantial. I lift my head. Realization. Not soil — water. I am in the river. My hand has snagged in an outgrowth of bushes.

My fingers tremble, curl, latch around a branch. The

muscles of my left arm tighten around broken bone, and I drag myself against the current. My legs kick, edge downward through the water until my feet find solid ground. Tension in my back; I straighten and stand; the eddy of the river threatens my balance. Staring down through the water, I order one foot then the other forward until I am on the bank.

Beyond the trees the night sky alters. The sun rises indistinctly behind a curtain of clouds. Crimson seeps through the gray. The sun climbs higher. The color deepens, arches overhead, spreads from horizon to horizon. No blue skies or even gray clouds; no normal dawn. I turn from the sun and seek out the town under a sky liquid with blood.

O

Fear cloaks the town by the time I reach it. From all around, I sense the dread. Voices buzz in my mind, spreading terror to those who have not yet witnessed the scarlet sky. My heightened perceptions search for guilt or remorse, some vestige of penitence. No one dares contemplate last night's deed; they have rejected the incident from conscious memory. Frightened, the town refuses to connect my murder with the dark red day.

O

The woman twists and pulls strands of her long gray hair around her skeletal fingers. Her yellowed eyes reflect the hazy, burning orb lodged among the streaks of red clouds.

"Nuclear holocaust?" She quizzes herself. Will she find the answers? "Total collapse of the ozone?" She shakes her head, making a feeble cross over her chest. "No — no — the retribution of God!"

She sets the transistor radio on the coffee table to a news station, but the voice drones mundane accounts of ecological poisoning, economic disasters, prejudice and strife. Not one phrase about itchy fingers pushing The Button. Not one mention of Atmospheric Catastrophe. Not one word about the Apocalypse. Her thin frame convulses under her striped dressing gown.

"Alone. Alone! in the vermilion darkness." She stumbles back from the window. "What should we do? What have we done?" She paces, her face wild. "What should we *do*? What have we *done*?"

The announcer's voice shrills out distant world events. Hands twitching, she picks up the transistor radio, carries it into the kitchen, drops it into the sink. With sharp nods of her head, she secures the drain plug and turns on the water. Sparks crackle under the spray. She turns back toward the living room and halts.

"Who are you?"

Her calm surprise at my presence is genuine. She has been unaware that I have watched her for so long. Coiling that dry hair around her fingers, she walks toward me. Her face creases with concern.

"Were you in an accident, young man?" she asks. "You look badly hurt. Should I call Doctor Olsen? I am a teacher and know some first aid." Her gaze skims over me, locks on my face. "But I don't think I can do anything about your eye. It seems quite put out."

"Mrs. Fletcher," I manage. My thoughts are as confused as hers. I am propelled by a mindless desire to touch the people of this place who touched me, who kicked the life out of my body. I reach out my hand; two blackened fingers hang limp and useless. I take hold of her bony wrist.

My touch jolts her. Her eyes widen, and for a moment her

mind is a black and white tapestry displayed for my viewing. I scan the occurrences of her life. In a low corner I find the link that has brought us together. She discovers it at the same instant. Whatever madness the red day has brought her breaks with recollection.

"Richard!" she gasps. She struggles against my hold, a writhing crone with a thatch of gray straw hair framing a skull face grimacing terror. "Richard! What have I done! What shall I do!" Her words screech to incoherency as she tries to pull herself away from me. My grip will not be loosened. Sputtering, whimpering, she sinks to her knees while I watch her mind implode with insanity. I leave her, a puddle of deranged humanity, on her kitchen floor.

O

A muddy path leads to the house on the edge of a steep hill. The chipped paint, the hanging screens, the crooked TV antenna, and the gutted cars remind me of past life. I step onto the loose boards of the narrow porch. The familiarity buffets me with images that weaken my purpose. Musty sounds of memory haunt me, faded smells seem fresh once more as I wrench open the door and walk into the dark kitchen. This was the home of my childhood. But had the stove been so crusted with old food? Had the sink been so scratched and stained?

Dishes and beer bottles litter the living room. The lampshades list above corroded brass. I grew up in this house, but my mother, even in poverty, would not have allowed this filth. I edge through the living room toward the back hall.

I realize that someone else I know now occupies this house. I twist the doorknob of what I remember as the master bedroom. The furnishings inside are the same, but the black-haired woman cowering in the corner is not my mother. She clutches a small boy to her sagging bosom and bloated stomach. She stares at me with watery eyes, her lips quivering over rotted teeth. Charlene — my brother's wife. I study the boy, Jake: he kicked out my right eye.

They know why I am here.

I am struck from behind, the force severe, the pain dull. I stumble against the bed, face my assailant — another nephew — what is this one's name? He brandishes a baseball bat; his fear makes him ferocious. I grin. He cannot hurt me. The greatest harm has already befallen me. I remember his face among the others last night; I advance. He swings the bat; I deflect the blow with an already broken arm. He attempts to escape; my fingers tangle in his long hair.

He is an easy kill.

I let the ragdoll body thud to the floor. I turn on Charlene and Jake. I nudge them with my foot. The boy squeals; mute with dread, Charlene gasps. With calm rage, I kick them.

O

Methodically, I work my way toward the abandoned section of town. One by one I find my murderers to exact my revenge, ruthless and uncompromising, for not one of them, even at the sight of me, can muster a shred of remorse. In their eyes, I was never human, never really a part of the town. They fear only for their own lives. Merciless, I forge a path of death and madness under the quiet, beautiful trees.

O

Memory has coalesced by the time I reach the dark house with the paintless fence; only a few strings to the past are yet unravelled. I am still driven to find the people who were present at my death, but now specific faces hang before me, faces of the people I hold most responsible. Like Alex.

My convertible sits outside the fence. I drag my hand with the two broken fingers over the smooth, shiny fender. My attention is caught by a dark stain on the white upholstery — blood. I look at the house. The torn screen door hangs open.

The smell of beer and sweat lingers in the air; I associate the stench with the past and the person who abused me after my parents' deaths.

"Wasn't right of him comin' here showin' off his money." Alex's words resound from the far end of the hall when I enter the house. "Couldn't let him come here spreadin' god-knowswhat in our town."

I edge down the hall. This house is familiar, but death has warped its connection to me.

"You'll still be safe here," Alex continues, his tone accented by alcohol. "You're part of the town. Mind your business like you done before and you'll be safe."

His broad figure backs into the hallway. The sweaty hair mats his skull. His shirt is tucked tightly around his swollen stomach. He hitches up baggy gray pants.

"Keep your mouth shut and you ain't got nothin' to worry about."

I tap Alex on the shoulder. He turns, a look of mild surprise on his face. In his drunken stupor, he reacts sluggishly. The thick lips slacken, the mouth drops open. The heavy eyebrows twitch, rise to reveal bloodshot eyes. He staggers against the door frame, then retreats along the hall toward the back of the house.

His fear fuels me. Like the others, he knows only the horror of my presence. Instead of remorse, I sense righteousness. His thoughts are a black slate with cruel names scrawled across it. He sees me as a plague rat to be skewered and burned.

I pursue him. He crashes into the kitchen table, runs for the door. His fat hand fumbles with the delicate key in the lock. I grab his collar, twist it tight, and drag him back. With ease, I throw him headlong against the refrigerator. He crumples to the floor. Groaning, he pushes to his hands and knees, glances over his shoulder. Blood runs into his eyes. I take a step toward him; he scrambles toward the hall. I reach for a weapon, pick up a full beer bottle. The thick glass makes a perfect cudgel; I strike him on the back of the neck, and the glass does not break . I bring the bottle down again, drive him to the floor. I bludgeon him.

I glimpse movement in the hallway. Silhouetted against the red light streaming through the front door, a man stands watching. He, too, was at the scene of my death. I lift the dripping beer bottle high and smash it into Alex's skull. Bone shatters; blood splatters in glistening drops across the tile. The man flinches; a hand pressed against each wall, he backs down the hall. Clutching the beer bottle, I stalk him.

Waves of helplessness wash over me from this man. I am confused. The others have known the futility of escape, but I feel a nuance of emotion that would have been foreign to anyone else in this town.

Shaking his head, the man stops at the entrance to the living room. Back pressed against the door frame, he sinks to the floor. A shaft of crimson light shines in his black hair. The left side of his face is bruised; red welts scar his shoulders and chest. The green eyes that stare up at me reflect not terror but sorrow. He lifts a hand toward me.

My fingers flex around the neck of the beer bottle. The

urge to destroy wells from deep inside. Possessed, my arm rises; the shadow of the bottle falls across his tear-streaked face. Resigned, he waits for the blow, his gaze locked to mine.

A voice I cannot place resounds through my mind. I hesitate. The voice murmurs my name with affection; the voice cries out in dread for my safety; the voice belongs to this man.

Scenes of remembrance glimmer before me. This man as a boy, laughing, whispering secrets. This man as a boy leaning out of a window in the middle of the night, fighting tears, fighting words that would take him with me out of a world of darkness and into a world of light and hope. A final tableau — this man lying in my arms and vowing, without words, that he will be with me forever.

I glance between the beer bottle, slimed with my brother's blood, and James's face, etched with grief. Sound quavers in my throat, erupts in a roar of agony and loss. I whirl away from James and heave the bottle. It explodes against a wall, mottling the faded wallpaper with red foam.

O

I flee James's house, for the lure of vengeance goads me. I do not know the extent of my control, and I must escape the temptation to harm him. My name, in his inflection, pursues me. I stagger through the town, venting my rage on any hapless soul who strays into my path.

The gas station stands before me. Through the discolored glass I see Carl's wide face. I lumber forward, strength deserting me. At the rusted pumps, I pick up the gas hose. I watch Carl's expression as I spray the building with gasoline. I find little satisfaction in his pleas for mercy. I am tired, ready to rest, but I must complete what I have begun.

I lay the gushing nozzle on the ground, watch the gas

splash against the bottom of the office door. Backing away, I take out my Dunhill cigarette lighter. I turn the flame up full, drop it, and walk away.

O

Sitting under a tree, I wait for the dusk of this dark red day. Not far away, the burning gas station streaks the sky with yellow flames and black smoke. From throughout the town echo the moans and cries of the mad. I smell the death, see the bodies that litter the street, but I am unmoved. The passion for revenge has been spent and forgotten.

James wanders through the remnants of the town. I sense in him an exhaustion as great as mine. What he has seen has drained him of horror and sorrow. I have robbed him of whatever compassion he would have felt for these people, these people who have never harbored compassion for us.

He kneels beside me. My destruction of the town has not completely crushed his capacity for emotion. I cannot bear the pain in his eyes as he studies me, and I turn my disfigured face away. The familiar silence hangs between us. Now there are no words that will ever ease it.

A streak of pale blue inches through the red of the sky. The moon rises from behind the opulent trees. The frail light arches over the town, softening the cold shadows, stilling the restless cries of the damned.

James moves closer, touches my shoulder. I look at him a last time before I shut my eye and lean into his arms, smooth and warm.

WHO COULD ASK FOR ANYTHING MORE?

Suburbia. Peace and quiet. Home of Mom and Pop, apple pie, and the boy next door. Late-model cars in driveways that border emerald green expanses of lawn. Majestic, leaf-laden trees lining black river streets. NFL on the television every Sunday and "As the World Turns" Monday through Friday afternoons.

Suburbia. Perfection.

Who could ask for anything more? As the old song goes.

Two-story red brick house. Oak trim on the wide front porch. Skip the clichéd white picket fence. Bright flowers between sculptured bushes along the foundation. Back yard: Weber grill, aluminum and plastic lawn chairs, redwood fence vined with ivy.

Who could ask—

What's that?

Over there!

In the center of the green carpet is a patch of withered

brown on the fringe of gray.

Perhaps it is but a stray shadow from the cherry tree by the garage.

Who—

Ethan Webster, a frosty mug of beer in hand, strolls out the back door onto the redwood patio. Tall, dark, unforgivably handsome, well-defined pecs and ridged stomach beneath brown fur — every father's dream for his nubile son. Tight, sinfully revealing running shorts and legs that taper sensuously from hip to foot. Maybe for every father's eldest, recently divorced son.

The boy next door grows up.

Setting the mug on a glass-topped, wrought iron table, Ethan lounges on a chaise, stretching sinuously for the beating summer sun. From beneath the chair, a copy of *Modern Romance*. Laugh away the afternoon with the flutter-heart crowd.

"He pushed me backward onto the bed. I could not restrain him. My gaze became riveted to the black hairs on the back of his hands as he roughly unbuttoned . . . ."

Perhaps it is *True Confession* after all. Father may want this one for himself.

Ethan reaches for the beer mug, wipes the condensation across the crotch of his running shorts, and smiles wistfully at the sensation and the activities of the hairy hands in his magazine.

His concentration is broken by movement in the neighboring yard. A wave of perfect blond hair on the breeze. A tanned hand smoothing it back into place. Martin. Ethan knows him as neighbors know neighbors — viewed through an open blind in the middle of the night. Ethan returns to his beer.

What's that?

Over there, in the center of the lawn. That gray patch.

Too far from the cherry tree to be a shadow.

Ethan sets aside mug and magazine. The perfect face is crinkled with confusion. The lawn was emerald perfection at seven this morning.

Investigation is required here, and Ethan is just the man for it. He takes the mug of beer for support.

Definitely a gray patch, bordering on black at the roots. Swigging beer, Ethan kneels, brushes his hand across the gray stands of grass. He jerks his hand back. Prickling, gritty feel to the grass. Unnerving. He wipes his fingertips against the green grass and jerks his hand back again. The same feeling, not as defined, not as unnerving. But there. He sets down the mug, braces himself, and pushes back the green. The blades run green, brown, gray, black at the base. Ethan grimaces, wipes his hand on his shorts.

What the hell is—

"What's wrong with your grass, Ethan?" Martin's voice has an appealing, deep resonance. "I've never seen anything like that."

Ethan stands, picking up his beer mug, and turns to Martin. His smooth, tanned arms are crossed casually atop the red-wood fence. The blond hair contrasts pleasantly with his bronzed face, itself the perfection of most boys' — men's, the look in those green eyes was never meant for any mere boy — gasping midnight fantasies.

"Neither have I," Ethan replies. He glances down.

At the edges of the patch, brown is enveloping green, and the gray invades with thin tendrils. Black spreads through the gray.

"My gardener is coming later," Martin offers. "I could ask him to look at it."

"That's very generous of you, Martin. Most neighborly." Ethan smiles two perfect rows of white teeth. He holds up his mug. "Would you like a—"

Ethan tilts his head to the side to better examine his mug. His confusion twists to something more. The bottom of the mug is graying to black.

O

Evening on the tree-lined suburban street. Shadow boys play Rambo killers in the dusk. Girls re-enact the latest Alexis–Krystal confrontation. Forty-watt porch lights snap on, beacons for the children at large. An MOR radio station competes with "Family Ties" flickering in darkened family rooms. Dishwashers and garbage disposals hum their evening chores. Sprinklers whirl to life, drenching the marauding Rambos.

The two-story red brick house with oak trim is dark, silent. On the redwood patio in the back stand Ethan and Martin.

Before them the brown-gray-black patch festers and engulfs the lawn.

"Dinner was delicious," Martin says, pushing long blond hair from his smooth face. "How did you do that to the chicken?"

"I'll give you the recipe," Ethan replies. He sips from his acrylic wine glass. "Do you think it will stop at the sidewalk?"

A major concern. The sidewalk was just relaid at the beginning of the summer. Grass seed is cheap compared to pouring cement.

"The sidewalk is already dead," Martin says. "How could it kill it?"

His simple logic is getting on Ethan's nerves, but he is a neighbor, and his gardener did examine the patch — when it was much smaller. Ethan will allow Martin an excess or two.

"What about the house?" Ethan wonders aloud.

In the same deadpan, deep resonance, Martin answers, "The same."

Ethan gulps the last of his wine. A sure nerve steadier.

"The cherry tree is going to go, however," Martin comments.

The patch has almost reached it. In the evening breeze, the cherry tree quivers its branches. Frightened of what is to come. A cherry jiggles loose and falls, quite slowly, Ethan thinks, to the grass.

plop. Just like that, lower case. plop; and the gray swarms over it and the black comes at the gray's heels until the cherry has melted into the ground. Leveled out, flattened. Gone.

"You see," Martin says, looking up at Ethan's profile.

You see. Damned irritating, that's what Martin really is. Sooner or later, Ethan will learn not to associate with neighbors, especially perfect blonds who inhabit men's fantasies.

"It'll probably take the redwood fence, then start on your flowers, then your grass and those jade bushes," Ethan says. Revenge.

Martin turns toward his yard.

Yes, sweet, delectable revenge.

What's that?

Sound, we have sound.

Crackling. Crackling from the

Sidewalk.

Terrific. It's going to take out the sidewalk as well. Next will be the patio, maybe the garage, then — last but most

— the house. Seventy thou brown-gray-blacked out of existence.

The patch chisels at the concrete. First just a sliver, then a chunk. The brown goes first, weakening; the gray comes next, chipping; last the black stretches onto the sidewalk. Ragged veins pop and split the concrete and the fragments powder to the dirt underneath.

"This is really distressing," Ethan exclaims. He drops the acrylic wine glass, and it bounces across the redwood, rolls toward the edge of the patio. Ethan marches toward the steps, but Martin grabs his arm and jerks him back.

The wine glass topples over the edge.

No sound.

"Maybe we should go inside," Martin suggests.

Ethan pulls free and creeps to the edge of the patio. The wine glass is slowly sucked up by the patch.

Beside him, Martin says, "Or maybe for a long drive. A really long drive."

O

Wee hours of the morn. Moms in rollers and cold cream, Pops in soiled underwear sleep at opposite sides of kingsize beds. Children curled under GI-Joe and Barbie sheets dream Chuck Norris and Bo Derek realities behind faces of fragile, transitory innocence. Houses creak on their foundations, something scuttles behind locked basement doors, a Harley roars in the distance.

The darkest hours of time.

The two-story red brick house looks like the others on the street. But don't look in the back yard. The grass and sidewalk are gone. The garage is crumbling; the patio lists on sinking supports. The cherry tree is bent and toppling.

Yet, the patch has stopped growing. The boundaries of its domain are temporarily set; this small section of suburbia will satisfy it for now.

New developments are on the wind.

Ethan stands in the kitchen, his enviable body cast blue by moonlight seeping through sheer curtains. He watches the back yard through the screen door while he pours beer into a mug. A new mug — the other, claimed by the patch, has been sacrificed to it. He is alone in his vigil. Martin had wanted to stay, but Ethan sent him out the front door, before the curious looks of the curious neighbors. Still, Ethan suspects that Martin is yet awake and watching, like him, the lull in the patch's advance.

And it is but a lull. Ethan knows that. The moment the splintering collapse of the patio ceased and the first traces of odor reached him, he knew that the spread of brown-gray-black was only in check. Something different will now occur. He knows it as he instinctively knows every inch of himself.

The smell is abruptly stronger and rank. A gray mist seeps from the black; frail wisps rise on still air.

Ethan drinks his beer and waits.

Rumbling. From deep down. Under the back yard.

Even the tiled floor beneath his bare feet trembles, sends vibrations through his body. Apprehension is shaken free. Ethan sets down his beer mug and considers flight.

The ground at the center of the yard trembles. Just a bit. A bit more. More. The earth quakes, and the dirt crumbles downward into the ground, siphoned down to the source of the rumbling. But now the rumbling is a bass roar of under-ground thunder.

The windows rattle. In the china cupboard, plates and

cups and saucers clank. Pots and pans clatter off the drain-board and bounce across the tile against Ethan's feet.

Flight is forgotten. Dreadful fascination holds him in the kitchen. Mechanically, he lifts his beer mug, swigs more brew, then sets the mug back on the counter.

"*Ethan* . . . ." The resonance of Martin's voice is thin and quavering. "Is it an *earthquake* . . . ."

The back yard is sinking at the center; the pit is ever widening. The mist has churned itself to a full-fledged fog that wraps itself around the cherry tree, caresses the redwood fence and the garage.

Right, Martin. Pretty funky earthquake.

Against pleas of common sense, Ethan opens the back-door and steps onto the listing patio. Not completely deaf to reason, he clings to the door frame with one hand. Across the redwood fence, he can see Martin's face pressed against the screen of his kitchen window.

"*Ethan* . . . ."

"No earthquake," he says, his voice quiet, but Martin hears him over the increasing detonations beneath the yard. "This might be a good time for you to go for that ride."

"What are you going to do?"

The patio heaves. Christ, the whole house and yard and street and neighborhood heave.

Ethan falls against the doorframe, sees Martin tip side-ways out of the frame of his window, his blond hair a trailing scarf. He grabs the doorframe with both hands as the earth tilts the other way. His feet slip from under him; he crashes to his knees, but keeps hold of the door frame. No way is he going to fall into the brown-gray-black. The far side of the patio collapses. He hangs by his hands on the incline. The vibrations — violent, unceasing — rack his body.

The pit has ripped open the yard to where the expensive sidewalk had been. And the brown-gray-black is again on the move. It flows over the edge of the patio and toward Ethan's dangling feet.

"Ethan!"

He scrambles up the patio, his feet slipping, splinters cutting into his flesh. The black speeds up, climbing closer. He throws himself through the kitchen door, jumps to his feet, and jerks shut the screen door.

"Ethan!"

He cannot see Martin. All he can see is the black waiting but a pace from the door, the trembling ground, and the growing pit.

He senses the next attack and flips the lock on the screen door. Everything pitches toward the back yard. He topples against the screen, but the lock holds. The china cupboard skids across the floor and thuds against the wall beside him. The dishes cascade out and shatter against him.

The fence between his and Martin's yard rattles, nails popping, boards cracking. The black climbs the fence as it collapses and the patch invades Martin's yard.

"Ethan—"

"Get out!" he shouts back. "Get the hell out!"

"What about you?"

"I — I don't know . . . . Just go!"

The black on the patio quivers, inches forward, seems to study and assess him.

"Ethan, it's crawling up the house—"

"Get out!"

Arms of brown-gray-black skitter across the patio, circling

the threshold. Yet, it does not attack. He is vulnerable behind the thin screen, yet—

"It's coming through the screen!" Martin wails. "E—"

Like a tape recorder turned off, Ethan muses.

On the patio, the brown-gray-black titters in amusement.

In the yard, where the pit has reached its zenith of circumference and darkest depths, what started as the gray fringed brown patch evolves once more.

Some sort of creature — not creature exactly — creature is too sweet a word to describe what is emerging from the wide, black pit.

Scales — drool — and teeth.

Brown — gray — and black.

No minions of Hell these. Far worse.

Brown-gray-black assaults the screen door.

Ethan jumps back, swings shut the wooden door with its slit of window. Twists the key; throws the bolt.

The beasts from the pit drone across the black and throw themselves against the house. Some dart toward Martin's; others slither into unsuspecting, sleeping suburbia.

And the pit begins to glow. And from the glow rises a shadow. And the source of the shadow shatters Ethan's mind.

O

My home is a patch of green. Night and night I sit on my green grass while purple-red clouds swirl the sky and brown-gray-black rules suburbia. Snapping yellow lightning chars the air.

There is no day.

My neighbors are beings of scales and drool and teeth and fire eyes that scorch life. They leave me to my patch of green.

I am pet Ethan, and this is Chaos' domain.

Destruction. Carnage. Shattered buildings; blasted cars; gnarled trees. Oozing slime and fissured earth.

Who
Could ask
For anything
More?

HELL IS FOR CHILDREN
Cruising with Andrew — Again

I

I wake up late and piss and moan about the cold. I am always cold — even at the height of summer I have a definite chill about me. Staggering into the bathroom, I plug the tub, twist the handle crowned "H" and — jump back. I hate running water.

Of all the things on this planet, I hate cold, running water, and sunlight most.

Well . . . . I can think of a few others, but how many people nowadays wear large silver crucifixes and tote wooden stakes and mallets in their backpacks?

The tub full, the running water securely off, I sink down to my chin in the scalding water. Lost in the wet steam, I open my mind to the swirl of memories. Sunlit beaches, Sunday afternoon shopping sprees at the Mall, Italian food.

Then a face — stone cold and compelling — finds shape in the contours of the haze. I shut my eyes and slip under the water. That memory — can it be five years old? — I can live without.

O

Have you ever tried getting dressed without a mirror? Wonderful results — crooked ties and standing collars. Worse —try buying clothes without the aid of a mirror:

Excuse me, salesperson, does this jacket hang right in the back?

There's a mirror—

Just answer the question, Airhead.

A wooden pain in the chest. It is hard to be a sharp-dressed man if you never see yourself full on.

I do not even want to discuss the rigors of shaving or drying the hair.

I grope at my ensemble. Everything feels right. From the chest down, everything looks — oops. ZZZZip up the slacks, Andrew. The world is cold enough without freezing life's essentials.

Wallet, jacket — customized onyx-handled switchblade — keys, and a cassette for the road.

One last chore—

CLUNK falls the lid. Bed's made.

I'm outta here.

O

I wade through the tide of college students that ebbs and flows over the sidewalks of the Village. The fall session has started, and the sea is full of new faces and new possibilities — new challenges for the old dilemma. Swept up in their intoxicating heat, surrounded by their ephemeral beauty, I allow the undertow to drag me toward the boutique. I have four hours of nightshift to face before I need to grapple with the dilemma.

– 93 –

The waves part, depositing me in front of a row of newspaper vending machines. With a few minutes to spare, I scan the day's headlines — and freeze.

I am in the news.

Body Count Rises in Decapitation Killings

I would think that the head count is rising as well and purchase a paper to find mention of it. Ah, yes, here it is. Heads.

Waitwaitwait. This cannot be correct.

The heads of the last six victims of the Sleepy Hollow Killer (newspaper people are so clever) *have yet to be recovered.*

What kind of game is this? I distinctly remember leaving the heads with the bodies.

Someone tugs on the tail of my jacket. Startled, I toss the newspaper to the sky; the pages flutter around me. Someone giggles. I put on my most serious face and turn. Kevin is not the slightest put off.

"Why so jumpy, Andrew?" this child-man manages between titters. He picks up the front page and jabs a slender finger at that headline. "Afraid you'll lose your head over someone?"

He who giggles loudest, giggles last.

My hand slips into my jacket pocket. The switchblade — eight inches of razor-sharp blade — waits patiently.

"Aren't we late for work, Kevin?"

How easily eighteen-year-olds are frightened. Kevin glances through the wide windows of the boutique to the pacing store manager. One of this quarter's freshmen and only recently employed by the boutique, Kevin's position is precarious. I, on the other hand, am an employee of long standing and can afford a few minutes' tardiness.

This boy's hot little hand clamps around my wrist. He drags me toward the boutique as if both our jobs depend on immediate arrival.

"Not too late," he mutters. "It's only—" He consults his watch. Am I hallucinating or is there a superhero flying across the watch face? "It's only two minutes past."

We navigate the crowd to the boutique doorway. Glancing at me, Kevin shakes his head and stops.

"Andrew, do you get dressed in the dark?"

My turn to be unnerved. Did I fasten my stickpin through my skin and not notice — again?

On tiptoes, Kevin reaches up and tucks my shirt collar under the lapels of my jacket, removes the stickpin — it is upside down — and, fingers brushing scaldingly against my throat, replaces it.

"You're an enigma, Andrew," he says, stepping back to survey me. His gaze lingers a bit low a bit too long. "Everything else looks dandy." Blushing, he giggles and runs inside.

Insecure, I touch the stickpin, then follow in his warm wake.

O

The heads of the last six victims of the Sleepy Hollow Killer have yet to be recovered.

This news haunts me more than my usual dilemma as I roam the streets after midnight. Who would be sicko enough to snatch the heads of my marks? More important than *who* is the big WHY. Headhunters in this college town? — I kinda be doubtin' it. I glance around, memorizing the faces of the other stragglers. Is one of them the head-thief? Does one of them know who — and what — I am?

A headlight beam slices across me, playing hell with my

vision. Sputtering like a sick lawn mower, a Honda scooter whips up to the curb beside me.

"Need a lift?" Kevin asks — and giggles.

I keep walking. "No, Kevin, I don't need a lift. I have a car. People my age drive cars."

He keeps pace — and keeps giggling between words. "Then why are you walking?"

"People my age like to walk once in a while as well." I had not realized that walking had become old-hat.

"Want a lift back to your car?"

Oh, the temptation to cut that giggle short.

Ahead I see refuge. A bar — no one under twenty-one, thank you. I make a beeline. The scooter engine revs. Kevin catches the sleeve of my jacket as I veer toward the neon beer signs.

"I can't go in there." No giggle. I did not realize an eighteen-year-old could look so serious. I suppress a wicked smile.

"I come here every night after work for a drink."

Seriousness to confusion. "No, you don't."

I pull my sleeve free of his grasp, edge toward the door of the bar. He has been following me. I am reminded of Brett — Brett of the compelling face. He followed me nightly five years ago. I study Kevin's face closely, search the eyes for the demon I had once seen in Brett's. Perhaps this child-man is capable of head-napping.

"Well, you don't." He squirms under my scrutiny.

"Well, I am tonight." I turn toward the bar and toss "See you at work tomorrow" over my shoulder before I go inside.

A final image framed in the bar's doorway: Slumped on a Honda scooter, a short, thin child-man, rejected and dejected, gazes off into space, his long blond hair pulled by the nightwind.

O

I choose a corner table, *sans* view of the door, and settle in with a margarita — strawberry, my favorite. Ignoring the rambunctious patrons, I stare into my glass and see those six missing heads floating in the red slush. I recall every face and try to connect them to body and location of final ecstasy. The hills above town still offer the perfect seclusion for my trysts, but when the mood strikes, I enjoy an invigorating encounter down at the beach — stiff ocean breeze and frenzied spray of the surf. As much as I hate to admit it, either setting provides ample cover for spying head-hijackers.

I stir my margarita; the six heads, caught in the whirlpool, sink. I take a sip, grimace at the sweet bitterness, and survey the liquor-soaked boys frolicking through the layers of cigarette smoke. Any one of them could be the culprit. Any one of them could have been in one of the bars I frequent. Any one of them could have trailed after my mark and me, and watched. I shudder. The idea of being observed in the height of passion does not appeal.

I gulp my drink — and nearly choke. I recover as gracefully as possible; at least I don't exhale red foam out of my nostrils.

"You all right, Andrew old boy?"

I nearly choke again. Who would recognize me? I rarely come to this place.

The bartender stands beside my table. He is svelte and well-appointed. I know where he shops; only our boutique carries those slacks and that tie. I reassure myself that he knows me from work, then I recall that he and I were in the same classes before the great alteration of my life.

"Went down the wrong pipe," I say, forcing a smile. Never ever pick up a mark here, Andrew. This one will remember.

The bartender — what the hell is his name? — hands me a folded piece of paper. "Communication from the real world."

Under his scrutiny, I read the note. In the hand of a child trying very hard to write like an adult: "Drink faster. It's getting cold."

I shove the note into the same pocket as the switchblade. I really don't need this kid in my life right now.

"Another margarita, please."

"Is that your answer?" the bartender — Steve, that's it! — asks.

"Answer?"

"He requested an answer." A smile, crooked and nasty. "I have one for him if you don't."

"Tell him it's past curfew." And keep your other ideas to yourself, Airhead.

He gapes at me as if I am the biggest fool on Earth, shrugs, and goes to deliver my message.

Shanghaied heads and persistent babies — what other joys does the night offer?

O

Reaching for a semblance of conformity, I make the requisite trip to the facilities. One cannot down strawberry margaritas all night and not hit the head. People stare at you, waiting for your eyes to turn yellow. What's a few minutes at a urinal — hissing unobtrusively — to stave off jealousy? Who wouldn't die to avoid public restrooms?

And isn't this one the epitome of interior design and floral scents? I've seen better lit, more fragrant caves — believe me, I've hung out in quite a few.

Sidestepping a stream springing from one of the urinals, I

stumble against the door of a stall. The door swings open.

"Occupied, asshole," a gruff voice informs me.

"It was never my intention to join the party—"

Oops, Andrew realizes that there *is* a party in this stall.

A tall gent — with a rather regulation clone coif — stands with his back to me. The way his shirt is pushed up to his armpits gives me my first clue that this is not a solo act. The pair of hands, which cling to denim-wrapped curves that even Andrew could envy, provides the second clue. A closer inspection — another gent, don't I know you? — sits on the stool. Maybe I don't; I can't see his face too well.

The tall gent glances over his shoulder to scold me with flashing eyes set in an angular face. He shoulders the door shut.

I'm a voyeur at heart — so stake me!

Andrew could tell a few tales of his daylight years that would make this tryst small potatoes. But he won't. Too many memories in one night make the undead morose.

O

I indulge myself in three more strawberry margaritas. Not the same intoxication level achieved from the sustenance of my existence, but cloud floating eases the taunting of the dilemma and obliterates the worry about lost heads. And, believe it or not, it freezes out the hunger; no need to find a mark tonight. Tomorrow I'll trip out of town and satiate myself far from watching eyes.

Damn! Watching eyes.

Through the closing-time shuffle of frantic pairing, I discover that I am being cruised. I look away but cannot distract myself from that face, that body, and that attitude. This is, of course, bad news. I need to lie low around here for a while.

What good are resolves if you break them twenty seconds after they are made?

Time to go home, snuggle up in the cool satin, and shut the lid on another night. I drain my glass, stand, and realize I am staring at the cruiser again. For a moment I am mesmerized by the quick flutter of a strong hand over significant body parts. Even through the tequila haze I can decipher his suggestion. I allow myself a moment's contemplation.

Andrew, Andrew, I scold myself, where is your fortitude?

Andrew, Andrew, my lower regions coax, you can still have a good time without resorting to the switchblade.

While the two voices in my head argue it out, I walk to the bar rail. Steve, still incredulous over my reaction to Kevin's note, tallies up my bill. As I give him money, he clasps his hand around mine.

Instant reaction to the chill of my skin: He drops his gaze to my hand, then studies me closely.

"Getting sick, Andrew old boy? Your hands are as cold as death."

"Cold hands, warm heart," I retort, slurring the words beyond my drunkenness.

"Look, Andrew, go for the little boy," Steve says, lowering his voice to conspiratorial tones.

Do I look like I need advice, Airhead?

"So he's young. We're the same age, right? I'd go for him "

"I'm not up for the part of Daddy right now."

He laughs as he takes my money to the cash register. "You don't have to be. It works the same whether he's eighteen or twenty-eight." Then, returning with my change: "But there is a bit more responsibility involved. If you're in it for the long haul." He folds the change into my hand and winks. "Remember, Andrew old boy, he's awfully adorable, and — if my guess is right — he worships the air you breathe."

I am tempted not to tip this big-mouthed airhead, then I abruptly shove three ones down the front of his slacks. Not waiting for a reaction, I forge a path toward the door.

The path is blocked by the cruiser.

The two voices in my head resume the debate.

The cruiser is taller than I; he has spent considerably more time with Nautilus. Yet, I find the roots of narcissism in his attraction: similar facial structure, the same dark brown hair, the same round brown eyes.

I smile politely and veer around him. I sleep with myself every day, and I am not in the mood to deal with my twin tonight.

This bastard is persistent.

"Was it something I said?" he asks, stepping in front of me once more.

That settles it; the man has no brains. Still, I play at diplomatic.

"No." I force a burp. "But I don't want to throw up on you." Such a way with people, Andrew. He backs away. "Nice shirt." I sidle around him and finally reach the door to the outside world.

Somebody please tell me I am hallucinating — please!

Across the street, huddled inside his cotton acrylic sports jacket, Kevin sits on his scooter. Chin on chest, he has fallen asleep — it must be hours past his bedtime.

Balanced on the edge of the curb, I study him. He looks even younger in repose, too innocent for the likes of me to even think about. No dilemma here. Yes, he is beautiful; that face deserves to be rescued from the ravages of cruel time, to be preserved for eternity. But he is — I remind myself — barely beyond childhood. He has not had a chance to find out about life and the tidbits of contentment it offers to a lucky few.

And what about the underbelly of life, Andrew? my nastier side quizzes from behind my eyes. Take him into the hills, have a good time, and spare him life's vicious cycle of repetitious boredom. Open the switchblade and do the child-man a favor.

I shiver, but the chilly night is not responsible.

Behind me, the bar patrons are being shooed into the street. The cruiser's aftershave wafts close at hand. Purposefully, I stumble off the curb, dangerously close to a passing car, then cross. Obedient for a change, the dilemma stays behind.

When I stop beside Kevin and his scooter, I am pinched by guilt. In his sleep, he trembles. He will probably contract pneumonia. For two hours, while I sat in warm comfort, snarfing strawberry margaritas, he has been waiting.

I place my hand on his shoulder; through his clothes, the heat of his skin against my palm reminds me of a vast gulf between us that has to do with more than age.

"Kevin."

He wakes with reluctance, squints at me without recognition.

"It's not safe to sleep in the street." Look who's handing out this warning.

His eyes widen as he forces his mind to focus. He smiles. "You're drunk." He picked up on that fast enough.

"And you should be at home. It's after two."

"Do you think they'd let me use the bathroom in the bar?"

First things first, I suppose. I walk Kevin across the street, explain to Steve the price of two-hour vigils in the cold night. After Kevin has gone into the bathroom, I turn toward the door.

"Why not wait for him?" Steve asks, ever the matchmaker.

Playing deaf, I walk outside. I see only the Honda scooter. I do wait; don't ask me why.

O

His slender hips scorch the insides of my thighs; his back against my chest is like sun-fired porcelain. The nightwind rushing around us keeps my mind clear as Kevin speeds the Honda scooter through the Village streets. After brief argument, I relented to a ride to the parking structure: the most compensation I can afford after he waited so long for me. Unfortunately, accepting the lift resurrected the dormant giggle.

Kevin veers into the parking structure at breakneck speed. I am certain we will crash; Kevin will be killed, and I will spend eternity mangled, the side of my head caved in. Miraculously, the frail little man keeps the scooter balanced, and we sputter up the ramp toward the top level and my car.

A dark silence, broken only by the whine of the scooter's motor. Uneasiness settles over me, and I search through the shadows as we buzz past one level after another.

And I swear a man lurks there, between those two square, graffitied pillars.

"Did you see him?" I whisper into Kevin's ear.

He shivers at my cold breath against his skin, but does not seem to hear me. He drives up the last ramp; I stare over my shoulder, certain that the head-burglar is here.

The scooter skids to a halt beside my Le Baron. Oh, yes,

Kevin knows my car without being told. Climbing off the seat, I wonder just how much about me Kevin does know.

"Buy a helmet if you drive like that all the time," I tell him. Naturally, he giggles at the suggestion.

"Now what? — Andrew?"

I am listening for other sounds in the parking structure, scanning for traces of another presence. My flesh tightens with apprehension.

"You go home, and I go home," I answer. How safe is it for him in this tiered, concrete cavern? "Follow me out, then don't follow me any more." I punctuate the last phrase with a reproachful stare that dampens Kevin's smile.

"Better yet, I'll follow you out," I say. If he is behind me, whoever is slinking behind the shadows could snag him without my knowledge.

"I have some beer—"

"Kevin, it's late. I'm drunk already, as you've pointed out. And I don't mix beer with margaritas. You go home, and I'll go home."

"All right," a bare whisper. He turns the scooter around.

I grab his arm; he looks at me expectantly.

"Wait for me to follow you."

He glances around the vast emptiness; he has finally caught on that all is not as it should be. Hands flexing, he waits while I unlock my car.

I keep him in the headlight beams as we wind our way back down to the street. Uneasiness has thickened to dread in my stomach. Someone else is here, waiting, watching. I do not see him again, but I know.

At the street, Kevin waves, turns right, and speeds away. I remain a moment in the driveway, watching him. Then, after a last glance in my rearview mirror, I hit the gas and swerve left out of the parking structure — before I have the chance to see anyone coming after me.

All the way home, I wonder if every set of headlights behind me belongs to the head-snatcher. The fear does not leave until I have double-bolted my apartment door and sealed myself in my coffin for the day.

O

I am awakened by the telephone. I fumble with the locks, push up the lid. Freezing, I crawl out, wrap myself in my bathrobe, and stumble into the living room. The jingle of the phone pierces my tequila headache.

"Hello?"

A silent void presses against my ear.

"Hello?"

A released breath — a muffled voice: "Sunset, Andrew." Click and buzz.

Very deliberately, I replace the receiver. Very calmly, I walk to the front door and check the locks — still secure. Very panicked, I press my face into the sofa pillows and scream.

II

I stand before the bedroom mirror — why bother? one may well ask — dressing for work. As I snap snaps, button buttons, and zip zippers, I glare at the reflection of the coffin, lamplight gleaming off its pewter finish. For one crazy moment, I think the coffin will transform into a four-poster bed, the last years will be a silly nightmare, and I won't have to worry about abducted heads or sunset wake-up calls.

The wish remains unfulfilled.

I focus on the mirror where my reflection should be. Nonchalantly, I fuss with my hair, straighten my tie, and try to restore some cool, try to force disembodied heads and threatening phone calls from my mind.

Impossible.

I open the dresser drawer and take a revolver from under the stack of pastel socks. I study the weapon, which is loaded with silver bullets — I have been watching too much television and have an eccentric fear of werewolves. I strap on the holster, wedge the gun under my arm, and put on my sports jacket. Bless my departed soul — the concealed weapon does not interfere with the lines of my ensemble.

In the living room, I catch myself before I turn off the lights. Carrying a sofa pillow, I do a turn about the room, then posture a Vanna White beside a gargantuan Japanese television.

At certain points of my promenade, the shadow of the pillow stretched prominently across the thin drapes.

I have a marvelous idea.

I kill all lights. In the rocking chair before the front window, I set up two pillows. Scavenging through the coffee-table litter, I find the remote control command center and snap on the thirty-five-inch-stereo-with-surround-sound-color TV. Flickering blue light fills the room; reflected growls, synthesizer music, and screams pulsate from the eight-inch speakers. And on the front window drapes looms the hulking shadow of a man settled in for a night of television terror — white-washed families and butched-up detectives.

Norman Bates's mother has returned — again — to bamboozle my tormentor, whom I am certain is watching the building. I am free to ramble through the night.

I smile at my ingenuity, then pray that the head-napper

does not know that people of my — shall I say, persuasion — do not cast shadows.

○

Ever so cautious, I climb to the roof of my apartment building. Tonight, I am resorting to the old world mode of transportation. I cannot take the car if my charade is to succeed, and — to be truthful — I am more than reluctant to leave my car in the parking structure. Standing on the eaves, I hope a bat with a four-foot wingspan flying over the Village will not show up on radar. I jump.

Cooool — I'd forgotten how nifty this is. Nightwind buffets me like ocean waves on a summer's day. And the view — a vista of tree-crowned hills and shadowed valleys, sparkling lights of the town, shimmering water of the bay — spreads peacefully below for my singular pleasure. I veer above the glow and smog of the town and am tantalized by the unobstructed starfield. I soar, roll, dive, rise on the air currents. Everything is overwhelmed by the liberation found only in the night sky.

Yet, nagging responsibility beckons — bills will not flutter away on the breeze and work awaits. I loop the loop — one more time, Andrew! — and fly toward the Village.

The lights below dazzle, wink and blink red, yellow, green, white, lavender — a spectrum of infinity. The endless flow of students meanders through the winding, intersecting streets, counter-played against the current of shining vehicles. I make one more pass to offset the oncoming hours of assisting mindless bimbos choose their trend-setting wardrobes.

○

The alley, although a major thoroughfare, is deserted and I land, resuming my human form. Running a hand over my wind-cooled hair, rearranging my clothes, I take a step, falter like a drunk — too exhilarated to be earth-bound. I hear approaching voices and force myself to calm before heading into the street.

The row of newspaper vending machines in front of the boutique sober me. Six vanished heads tumble around me, raising bruises of worry.

Damn the head-thief and the trouble he has created.

At my entrance, the store manager nods. I search for my name tag among the assortment in the drawer below the cash register, then strain to see my lapel so that I can pin it on straight.

"Andrew, fix your tie," the store manager says.

"What's wrong with it?" I fumble at the thin strip of material.

"It's twisted." He swings his arm toward the mirror beside the dressing rooms. "We do have mirrors."

I have successfully avoided them for six years. I am not about to go stand in front of one now.

I cross the boutique, flattening my chin against my chest to better see the offending tie.

Kevin will fix it for you, a conniving voice whispers in my head. My gaze sifts through the boutique's customers and lights on Kevin. He is making a great show of arranging a stack of sweaters. He glances at me, then turns to assist a chesty number wearing jeans that are at least two sizes too small.

I stop near the mirror, careful not to get too close, and pretend to straighten my tie. A hand grabs my shoulder, swings me around. Glowering, the store manager slaps my hands down and tugs at my tie.

"Get with the program, Andrew. This is a fashionable, expensive joint. Our sales people should reflect that . . . ."

His litany goes on, unheard. He has pushed me into the range of the mirror. I stare at the glass. There is the store manager, his hands working at thin air, for all the world to see.

"You did not buy this shirt here, Andrew," the store manager continues. "I know every piece of funk we sell, and this is not on the roster." He stands back, gives me the once over. "But it does add a certain panache to the slacks." He starts to turn toward the mirror.

Panic.

"There's someone at the register," I practically scream, jerking him around. "Thanks for the help." I shove him toward the front of the store.

I stumble away from the revealing mirror and notice that Kevin is staring. I compose myself, smile. Kevin drops his eyes, pivots, and collides with his customer. Arms flail, sweaters and slacks scatter, and Kevin, the chesty number in the tight jeans under him, crashes to the floor.

"Sorry . . . . Let me help you up . . . ."

"'S'right. Let's do it again."

Kevin glances at me. In a moment, I read the thought behind those big blues. He is actually considering another tumble with the chesty airhead right here in front of God and all his children.

Well, isn't this just a fine turn of events, Andrew? What happened to the child-man who worshipped the air you breathe, the child-man who giggled at every insult you tossed in his direction?

You have been abandoned, Andrew, that is what has happened.

For what? An airhead with inflated pecs, a common pretty boy who has to wear jeans two sizes too small to accentuate what he does not possess.

The state of the world is not what it used to be, Andrew. Not at all. How easily they forget their idols. How easily alliances are formed and abandoned for the first set of tight buns that sashay through the store.

The mood of the night is set. The bliss of flight is forgotten. My mind settles comfortably into moroseness. I pass through the four hours of my shift as the specter that I really am — present but not a common reality. A dead man without a life in a world of warm-blooded clothes horses without a thought for tomorrow or yesterday.

Pass the garlic powder, please, I am feeling suicidal.

O

The internal midnight chimes take me back into the night. I exit the boutique furtively, not giving Kevin the opportunity to follow me. Andrew has no patience for children with wandering loyalties — even adorable ones with long blond hair and captivating big blues.

Of course, a sensible voice tells me, last night I did my best to brush him off, and he is hardly to be blamed for avoiding me.

I, however, am not feeling sensible, shrug off the voice, and remind myself never to take an eighteen-year-old seriously again.

More pressing dilemmas are at hand. Tonight I feel a nagging hunger rising — I can go only so long without at least a snack, strawberry margarita or no. Overlaying the hunger is persistent worry — where is the head-stealer? Was he fooled by the decoy I left at my apartment? I suspect that he is close at hand, roaming the night in my footsteps.

The two dilemmas twist around each other, a tangled, grotesque mass that transforms into a new question: Do I do a fly-by-night and seek my nourishment out of town, away from the possibility of yet another head being added to the MIA list?

Indecision drags me around the Village. I do not focus on the passersby, even when I sense that one or another of them has taken an interest in me. Contact on the street — albeit anonymous — is too dangerous. Weariness takes over. It is too late for a jaunt to the nearest hamlet. I veer off the sidewalk, following the trail of stragglers into a twenty-four-hour emporium that specializes in videos for the Bosco Society.

No sleaze joint this — all colored neon and chrome-glass shelves weighted with countless video boxes which are adorned with hunky boys and unbelievable titles. Equally hunky boys with unbelievable assets exchange covert glances in the aisles. I remember the game well: choose a mark, choose an appropriate title to transmit your delight. From there to the preview rooms or the privacy of personal domicile. Neither man nor title arouse much interest in me. I wonder if I am sick; this place is a gold mine of opportunity.

Much commotion at the doorway. Patrons scatter, but alas no escape is available. Several blue-uniformed, mustached guardians of law and order break through the barricade of employees. A mad dash by the boys in blue toward the preview rooms.

Have the police nothing better to do than harass the peace of this establishment? Are there not criminals enough on the streets? Is there not a head-pilferer on the loose?

My veins clog with panic. What if they search me? I have

an onyx-handled switchblade in my jacket pocket. Not good. Worse still: What if they arrest me? What will I do come dawn if locked up in a human cage? Ohyeahsure, I can pull the old transformation-into-mist-and-float-out-the-bars routine, but I am a rather upright citizen. I carry all the essential identification — I even have proof of auto insurance — in my wallet. I will be tracked down. A search of my apartment will prove illuminating to one and all. Who else in town has a pewter-toned coffin set between the bedroom nightstands?

Involuntarily, I back away from the sauntering uniformed clones and collide with the shelves. Several boxes clatter to the floor.

Terrific, Andrew, now they are all looking at you. And I am certain the expression on your face is all innocence.

The ringleader of this legal goon squad advances. His clipped mustache is edged with gray; the iron-gray eyes are framed by disapproving creases. His hand, all tendon and muscle, rests too easily on the butt of his revolver.

Revolver! Oh, sharpened stakes! I'm carrying a revolver loaded with silver bullets under my arm.

That's it, Andrew, the castle has at last been invaded by angry peasants. Hand out the stakes and mallets. Sleep eternal is at hand.

"Jittery little thing, aren't we," the ringleader says, giving me a sneerful once over.

The other patrons, frozen statues, look at the floor.

I strive to regain some dignity. I reject every answer that passes through my fevered brain. This is no time for a smart-ass remark, Andrew. Be cool. Take control.

"I slipped." Real cool. I am forever amazed at how inane I

become when I need to be profound.

"You could slip on the wet cement floors of the jail and crack open your pretty skull on the bars," he says in an even whisper. The statement is punctuated by a dead gleam deep in his eyes.

Perhaps this is the time to throw discretion to the winds and tear this bastard's head off his shoulders.

I could, too. And not even breathe hard.

Distraction. The raid has yielded a number of victims from the back rooms. In loud protest, they are ushered toward the door.

A young policeman, who looks as if he should be among the victims rather than the blue-boy terrorists, takes note of my situation. I wonder why he looks familiar.

He scans me briefly, then looks into the iron-gray eyes of his comrade. "We have our quota," the boy-in-cop's-clothing says. I feel as if this young one is ultra-aware of me. "Let's hit the bar up the street before calling it a night."

Salivating, they trail their prisoners out the door.

The unscathed breathe sighs of deliverance.

"This is chewing at my last nerve," one of the establishment's employees declares. Standing behind the counter, he is an interesting specimen with quarter-inch-long green hair and black-painted Mr. Spock eyebrows. "What happened to 'to protect and to serve'? This is the fourth damn raid this month!"

I share his indignance, if not his taste in personal beauty. A grumble rises from the other patrons, yet none of us storm the paddy wagon to free our brothers. A sad statement of the times. How much farther will we let them push us before we see an uprising like Stonewall?

Business as usual resumes. One marked difference: No one seems inclined to enter the preview rooms.

I stoop to pick up the video boxes I knocked over. A delicate pair of hands reaches down to help me. The hands are connected to a stunner with large hazel eyes, translucent complexion, and shoulder-length auburn hair. His smile flashes a too-perfect set of pearly whites.

"I guess we're the lucky ones," he says. "You especially. I thought they were going to nail you for certain."

Stake me is the phrase that comes to my mind.

I nod, unencouragingly. After the close call with the boys in blue, I am in no mood to face any dilemma. And this man is definitely the dilemma, from his head down to his itty bitty toes. I stand to put the video boxes back on the shelves; he mimics me.

"Are you all right?" he asks. "You're deathly pale."

What an uncanny sense of understatement.

"I need some air." I walk toward the door, ignoring the stare of the green-haired sales clerk. I have drawn enough attention to myself without branding my image into his brain with a departing smile.

On the sidewalk, the auburn-haired beauty and I stand side-by-side, silent; immobile. Down the street, the flashing lights of police cars pinpoint the site of another senseless raid. With little strain — one of the pluses of my existence is extraordinary night vision — I focus on the blue invaders. A billyclub slashes at one of the bar patrons. I recognize the assailant — the young policeman who, however unwittingly, saved me from exposure. Again I search my memory for the time and place I saw him before.

"It's a beautiful night," the auburn-haired man says,

pressing his arm against mine. "We could go for a walk on the beach."

Claxons resound through the brain. I search those hazel eyes for a reflection of Brett.

"Or we could go up into the hills," he continues. "I bet the view of town is—"

I back away. The beach or the hills. Who am I standing with? What does he know about six missing heads?

"Is something wrong?" he asks, his expression all confusion. A light comes on. "Bad idea! The murders—"

"Yes, the murders." He is my height and as thin — no excessive muscles or strength. That face holds the purity you find only in fairy tales. Yet, what strength, what visible signs of evil are needed to purloin the heads of my marks?

"I'm sorry," he says. "I've frightened you." The corners of his lips curl. "You can strip-search me for weapons if you want. At my apartment."

Brazen and cool. I nod. Inside me, hard calculation displaces trepidation. Andrew can play games, too. I trace a finger down the thin fabric of his shirt, over the contours of chest and stomach. I force a friendly smile.

"You're on."

He leads the way into a side street, dark and quiet. I keep in step, allowing his warm fragrance to stir the hunger. My hand is already comfortable around the switchblade.

O

We tumble across the bed, his body scorching my cold flesh. Although I perform with precision, my mind is focused on earlier images: his glassy stare, cryptic grins at my apparent fear of becoming the next victim of the Sleepy Hollow Killer. Mingling with these are flashes of memory, grainy black-and-whites of Brett with the compelling face and sculptured body. I easily equate the two as ghouls whose hungers are worse than mine. I rediscover the solution of five years ago — this beast must not live.

I enjoy his last moments. I will lead my tormenter to the ultimate ecstasy I bestow upon my marks before the hunger intercedes and the switchblade finishes the job.

He pins me to the mattress, his mouth at my throat — role reversal. From the corner of my eye, I see his hand groping toward the nightstand. His slender fingers fumble for something — an out-of-focus object obscured by the veil of auburn hair. I squint, stretch for a better view. I am rewarded with a flash of silver.

A crucifix.

Total role reversal. He plans to destroy me at the crest of our excitement.

A furious sound breaks from my throat. With an exertion of full strength, I flip him off the bed and toss him against the wall. I am off the bed, have the switchblade open in my hand before he hits the floor. In total rage I lunge, giving but a fragment of thought to the surprised terror in those hazel eyes.

We tumble across the floor, my switchblade probing his smooth flesh. Grunts of pain; geysers of blood. I wield my weapon well, in spite of his swinging arms and clawing hands. I pin him to the floor, my face at his throat, the switchblade groping under his ribs. He moans — a guttural sound of pleasure and agony, the linked extremes of existence.

Drugs! Damn the sun! He is pumped full of drugs. I rear back, disgustedly wiping his blood from my mouth. Add drugs to the list of things on this planet that I despise. I cannot feed on him, but I will end the plague of head-pillaging. I drive the switchblade into the base of his neck.

Done. Finished. I stand; my fury dissipates. My mind clears, but I still see red. Blood — blood is everywhere. I look down at my naked body — for pity's sake, just bloody everywhere. I stumble back from the corpse. Sickness wells within me. I have not seen such carnage since my first kill. Not even Brett's death was this messy — he had not struggled; he had enjoyed the final climax.

Time to split. I scramble around the room, sorting my clothes from his. My brand new slacks and shirt soak up the blood streaked from my chest down my legs. Ruined, and I haven't even got the bill for them. I sit on the edge of the bed to pull on my socks and shoes.

A flash of silver at my feet. I see through the shadows, and a new wave of revulsion seeps through me. I pick up the square, foil packet. Not a crucifix after all. I glimpse the body curled against the wall, the head in the corner.

Oops, I think I made a mistake.

O

Night flight is not so fun when the wind all but freezes your blood-matted fur. I spiral to the roof of my apartment building, nearly colliding with the air conditioner. Not my smoothest landing, but I am having a bit of trouble transmuting my claws back to feet. In future, I will not fly in such a frenzied state of mind. Lack of concentration could leave me with a left arm and a right wing.

It is late, but the building is teeming with obscure noises — popping water pipes, creaking floor boards, scurrying cockroaches — heightened to a cacophony of attacking blueboy airhead terrorists out to apprehend the Sleepy Hollow

– 117 –

Killer — me. I hesitate in the darkened hall, expecting one of my neighbors to round the next corner. The fear is not that I might get caught — although that is pretty high on the list considering the condition of my clothes — but that I will be forced to commit another senseless killing. One a night is plenty.

At last, the sanctuary of my apartment. The television still flickers over the pillow-man in the rocking chair; the eight-inch speakers still spew shrieking violins and piercing screams. Creeping along the wall, I find the remote and turn off the TV. I dismantle my decoy and stand a long time near the front window, tempted to peek into the street for some sign of the head-thief.

I reject the idea. What Andrew needs now is a nice hot bath and a calming, hunger-diverting margarita.

O

Clean, but hardly refreshed, I fill the tub with cold water and leave my clothes to soak. From there to the kitchen where I assemble the blender and gather the necessities for a nice, strong strawberry margarita. I rummage through the refrigerator. I swear I bought strawberries. All right, now we're talking. Not one to mess around, I make a two-blender batch.

Carrying the party-size pitcher and a glass into the living room, I settle on the couch. I down the first glassful — oh, that hazy chill from the stomach to the brain — before turning the television back on. The horror movie is still playing, and I try not to cover my eyes as the slimy, tentacle creature takes out a college campus.

The approach of dawn — and the marvels of tequila — leaden my eyelids. My grand *faux pas* of the evening tucked away for later guilt sessions, I head for bed.

Crossing the bedroom, I allow my robe to slip off my shoulders. In the morning I will regret leaving it on the floor, so far from reach, but right now I am too exhausted to care. Right now I am too exhausted to even shiver as the cool air embraces me. Ready to snuggle up in the warm closeness of my coffin, I push up the lid.

Wrongo, Andrew.

I am certain that someone finds this all too amusing for the comics, but Andrew is not laughing. To be perfectly blunt, I am on the edge of hysterical horror.

Fortunately, my present state of intoxication keeps the scream lodged in my throat, and I do not possess the strength to stumble backward over the furniture. I simply gape at the three heads, in varying states of decomposition, arranged neatly on the dirt that lines the coffin bed.

III

Dim sunlight filters through the thin living room drapes. The hard-edged shadows of furniture stretch across the carpet. Sounds in the quiet room — plastic scrapes wood; the bolt clicks back. The front door inches open to the limit of the chain lock. A pair of metal shears edge through the opening. SNAP! the chain is cut, and the door swings wide.

Alert, the man pauses in the doorway. He carries a large satchel. After a glance into the hall, the man enters, cautiously shuts the door. One step into the room. The floorboards creak beneath the carpet. He falters, his attention fixed on the door opposite him. A step at a time, he toes his way across the room, avoiding the creaks that would betray his presence.

The heavy bedroom drapes are drawn tight; the shadows

are a single dark mass. The man allows his eyesight to adjust. He isolates tiny details — the watch, the wallet, the switchblade on the dresser, the robe on the floor — before he focuses on the coffin set between the nightstands. Gripping the handle of the satchel, he advances.

The frail light from the living room picks out highlights in the pewter finish. The man places his hand on the coffin, then leans close, pressing his ear against the cold metal. After a heartbeat — two — he straightens, a smile on his lips. Setting down the satchel, he slips his fingers under the rim and pushes up the lid.

Within lies the naked corpse. Dark hair frames the angular face. The black eyelashes contrast sharply with the gray, waxen skin. The intruder scans the body — narrow shoulders, sinewy arms, long-fingered hands folded across the undefined chest, the flat ridges of the stomach. He smirks that the thin frame should support such an endowment.

Kneeling, the man opens the satchel and takes out his weapon: a two-foot-long crucifix, hand-carved of wood, its two-inch diameter tapering to a needle point. The man towers over the corpse in the coffin. He grips the crucifix at the crossbar, poises it briefly over the chest, then lifts it high.

Pounding — slow and steady — thunderous . . . .

The man hesitates, glances toward the living room.

THUD . . . . THUD . . . . THUD . . . .

O

I bolt awake, smack my forehead against the coffin lid. Through the colored dots dancing before my eyes hangs an image of a bloodthirsty, cross-shaped wooden stake. I try to slow my breathing. I wipe at the sweat that films my body. *Such a nightmare!*

A residual of horror, the pounding remains, distant and echoing.

Wake up, Andrew, the pounding remains because someone is knocking on your door.

Unlatching the coffin, I carefully push up the lid. Paranoid, I survey the bedroom. Nothing seems disturbed. I peek over the edge of the coffin to the floor. No open satchel, no abandoned wooden crucifix.

The knocking on the front door is insistent.

There lies my robe, out of reach. Shivering, I pounce on it, struggle my arms into the sleeves, and wrap what little comfort it offers around me.

At the front door, I peer through the peephole. Why am I surprised to see Kevin, his baby face and child-man body fish-eyed, in the hall? Something inside me stirs. I am actually happy to see the lad. I thought I had forgotten what happy meant.

The feeling does not last long. I never gave him my address. At some time, he has followed me to my abode. And he has the nerve to show up without even so much as a warning phone call.

I quietly unlock the door, jerk it open. Kevin jumps back, his eyes widen, his mouth drops open — a satisfactory response. Then, true to form, he giggles. I scowl, but the titter will not be squelched.

Is there a draft? I feel a definite breeze.

No wonder, Andrew, your robe is hanging wide open. You are giving the boy quite a show — for free.

I pull the robe around me and securely knot the sash.

"Do I get to come in?" Kevin asks, regaining composure and returning his gaze to my face.

"You'd better, so my neighbors don't think you're insane."

Delighted, Kevin bounces into the living room. Child that he is, he examines everything within reach. He gapes at the television.

"It's huge."

I wonder at his point of reference.

"What are you doing here?" I ask.

He strolls around the room, stops a few feet from the bedroom door. As nonchalantly as possible, I walk past him and pull the door shut.

"What's in there?" His face is aglow with mock innocence.

"The mortuary," I grumble.

"Ooo, we are in a lovely mood." Kevin plucks a piece of carpet lint from my robe. "Get up on the wrong side of the coffin?"

Is he following my lead, or does he know more than he should? I hope for the former; the latter would mean slitting that slender throat and defiling that fine blond hair with blood.

"You didn't answer my question," I say, gripping his shoulder and spinning him away from the bedroom. He saunters to the sofa and slumps among the pillows. I force down the response his smile arouses.

"I'm off tonight. You're off tonight."

"Convenient as hell, isn't it?"

"I thought we'd go out to dinner," he says. "My treat. After that—" He breaks into that giggle.

First reaction: throw the boy out on his ear. All right, I am hungry, but my fare is not offered on any menu that I am aware of. Then I make the mistake of studying Kevin closely. Beyond that wide grin, a plea resides in his big blues. Would it destroy me to spend one evening with him? Maybe over dessert I can probe for information about shanghaied heads. After that—

Andrew is such an old softy. I would probably be better off exposing myself to sunlight, yet I nod and say, "You're on."

Hand me my shades; he is beaming like a spotlight, giggling and squirming as if he has just been given an all-night spree in the Bosco Society Video Emporium.

"You sit still while I get dressed."

"Do you have anything to drink?"

I veer from the bedroom door toward the kitchen.

Kevin leaps off the sofa. "I can get it."

I intercept him, my hands on his shoulders. For no logical reason, his hands come to rest on my hips.

"Sit down. Watch TV. My home, I'll play host." Will I ever get past talking to him as if he were eight?

His hands are reluctant to release me, but he follows instructions fairly well. I walk to the kitchen doorway, glance back to be certain he is obedient.

As I cross the kitchen, the television blares, and I toss "Turn it down" back through the door. The sound spirals to a thinking person's level. What other inconsiderate or disgusting habits does he possess?

Don't think about it now, Andrew. That path leads to the dilemma, and you are not ready to contemplate its full implications in the case of Kevin.

After a quick glance over my shoulder, I open the refrigerator. I sort past the three heads in plastic ziplock bags and find a beer for Kevin.

O

After settling Kevin in front of the universal babysitter, I retreat to the bedroom and quietly twist the door handle lock. The three heads are sequestered in the kitchen closet, buried under an avalanche of grocery bags. If the child-man decides he wants another beer, he can help himself and not be startled by the leftovers I keep on hand.

I start my bath, then ponder my wardrobe. I choose suitably sedate attire for our outing. Nothing too seductive; Kevin has ideas enough.

Cocooned in the scalding water, I strive for a moment's peace of mind. Yet I am haunted. My sanctuary has been violated; I am lucky that the nightmare was just that. The possibility of awakening to a stake being plunged into my chest is distinct. If the head-thief got into my apartment during my absence last night, he could return during the day as easily as my dream-executioner. I make a mental note to rig a crossbar on the front door before dawn.

"Did you die in there?" Kevin calls through the bedroom door.

"Yes!" Quite truthfully — right here.

Giggle, giggle.

I climb out of the tub and bundle myself in the bathsheet. Do I seriously think that Kevin could be the head-snatcher? His remarks this evening could be as innocent as his round, smooth face — but is it coincidence that he has shown up on the heels of the presents I found in my coffin? He did seem terribly curious about the bedroom, but then, that could be hormones on the loose. Questions, questions.

A word of caution, Andrew — find the answers before you make another bad judgment call like last night's. You have already left one bloody trail, do not start another that will lead to centuries of regret.

Confident that I have put myself together in a presentable fashion, I unlock the bedroom door and join Kevin in the living room. The big blues are a tad glazed. Two empty beer bottles sit on the coffee table; he holds another between his legs. Laying my sports jacket over the chair, I carry the empties toward the kitchen.

"Hold on there, Andrew," Kevin shouts.

What — he wants me to schlepp the other bottle for him too?

A hot hand works its way into my back pocket and conforms to the curve.

"Something I can help you find, Kevin?"

With tantalizing slowness, he retracts his hand, smooths the back of my slacks. "Your pocket was sticking out. I never saw anyone have so much trouble getting dressed."

I face him. "My mind is on the big picture, kid, not the details." I back into the kitchen. From his expression, he will be sufficiently occupied with that one until I am ready to leave.

O

Nothing brings on the giggle faster than ordering a strawberry margarita in an Italian restaurant. Even the waiter — with that coif — has the nerve to raise an eyebrow. Let them smirk, let them giggle. Andrew is an individualist and will do as he pleases. Besides, the hunger chews persistently at my insides. If I do not get my margarita fix, I am bound to attack that morsel over there — ooo! better yet, that ruddy-faced one over there.

Returning with our drinks, the waiter demands our order. I am in a quandary. I am already a bit queasy from the odor of garlic that permeates the restaurant. Now I must select something to eat — how curiously will they stare when I ask if there is anything that has not been soaked three weeks in garlic?

I decide that the pasta and seafood salad — dressing on the side — might be safe. Kevin chooses sausages and peppers. He will be safe from me for at least a month. I will be lucky to be able to ride behind him on the scooter after we leave.

"Where did you disappear to last night?" Kevin asks. The candlelight lends a diabolical cast to his face. "After work. You remember last night, Andrew?"

"I went for a walk."

"People your age like to do that." He grins over his soft drink. "You didn't go to that bar. Your car wasn't in the parking—"

"Kevin, not to start an argument, but I would appreciate it if you didn't track my every move." Especially the decidedly wrong moves I made last night.

The hurt-little-boy look. "I just wondered . . . ."

In my most soothing tone, "I was tired. I went for a walk to unwind, then I went home."

"And slept until I—"

In my rudest tone, "Shall I keep a time log and turn it in every day?"

In the nick of time, the waiter arrives with our food. Uncomfortable, I sit back while the feast is laid out. These rollercoaster reactions to Kevin tear at one's inner serenity. Not that I possess much at this stage of my existence, but I had hoped this evening with Kevin would be calming, free of stress and strife. I cannot seriously believe that he is the head-burglar — there, I've admitted it — but neither can I have him trailing after me. If I wanted a puppy, I would buy one. Right now, what Andrew needs is a quiet evening without the intrusion of problems or responsibilities, and this conversation has created both. How do I solve the problems of his following me around without taking responsibility for scarring his child-man feelings?

"What did you have planned for after dinner?" I ask.

How the big blues light up. Even in the candlelight I see the blood rush to his face. He carves a sausage in two and twirls it through the marinara sauce.

Try another subject, Andrew, this one has left him with a mouthful of meat he cannot talk around.

Or perhaps that was his answer.

"Andrew old boy, what a surprise!" Steve, the bartender, slaps me on the back. With a jack-o-lantern grin, he hovers over our table. His thoughts are louder than his tie.

"Kevin, you remember Steve." I drip politeness.

Nodding, Kevin swallows. "My messenger to the sanctuary of the aged."

"I'm glad to see he hasn't left you out in the cold — again."

What a witty pair of airheads.

I take a bite of my salad — and grope for my margarita. Damn garlic! My personal entertainment committee is oblivious: Kevin and Steve babble on as only airheads do. I take the opportunity to re-arrange my food — I am quite practiced, and it looks as if I have devoured half the salad.

"Stop by the bar later, Andrew old boy," Steve suggests. "Bring the lad."

"Not a wise—"

"I'll reserve you a quiet, out-of-the-way table." Steve smiles devilishly at Kevin, pats me on the shoulder. "Rather conservative outfit for you, isn't it, Andrew?" He disappears into the restaurant's intimate, murky atmosphere.

Don't press your luck, Airhead. The night is long and the switchblade very sharp.

O

Steve has taken well to the role of Dolly Levi, providing us with a corner table away from the bedlam of boys on the go, attentive, personalized service that keeps our glasses full, and free strawberry margaritas. All that is missing is candle-light and 1,000 strings — somehow I know that if I asked, Steve would supply them. I find it all a bit much, but Kevin is drinking it up — an urchin set at the head of the palace table.

The margaritas have loosened Kevin's tongue, and he rambles tirelessly about college, work, and other mundane subjects that plague eighteen-year-olds. My ears follow his soliloquy while my eyes stray over the crowded barroom. I am still hungry, don't ya know, and the menu here is rich with delicacies. I single out prospective marks, eliminating those whose behavior speaks of drugs and those whose sheer beauty of presence would invoke the dilemma. In no time I have selected a dozen possibilities.

Of course, I would not think of approaching them while in the company of Kevin. I am not heartless — as a matter of fact, the heart is one of my few functioning internal organs. Nor would I hit a mark while Steve holds reign behind the bar.

And there is always the possibility that the purloiner of heads mingles with the crowd in hopes of adding another trophy to his collection.

A familiar face — a familiar flutter of a hand over significant body parts. The cruiser of two nights ago lounges against the bar rail, his round brown eyes trained on me. He trails the tip of his tongue eversoslowly along his shapely upper lip.

Maybe later, Airhead, when I've tucked the little man in for the night.

Which won't be too long from now. Kevin absorbs the margaritas like mother's milk. The big blues are networked with red, his smile is lopsided and overly congenial. His hand, which has found its way onto my leg, burns feverishly through my slacks to my cold flesh. His monologue is punctuated with long silences, his words slurred to some language I have never encountered. Yes, I do believe I should put the child-man to bed and turn my energies to more pressing needs.

Too late the decisions of the wise.

A hush falls, rippling from the front of the room. Patrons turn and part. My two favorite bashers in blue saunter through the crowd. From under the bills of their hats, their trained eyes search and probe for the slightest infraction against some outdated standard. The elder, with the clipped moustache and iron-gray eyes, veers toward the far end of the mahogany bar where two boys — brazen hussies — stand leg-in-leg. The younger of the cops, whose sharp features I still cannot place, struts through the smallest gaps between the petrified men and whorls of cigarette smoke. He glances this way.

And I remember that Kevin — all of eighteen — is drunk as a skunk at my side. I try to posture relaxation and innocence. From beside me, I catch a whispered "Hell's fire." Kevin has pulled himself together in a hurry. He deftly slides his empty glass in front of me, then produces a pack of cigarettes and lights up. The pose, if not the face, reeks of all of twenty-two.

I glimpse Steve, tall and rigid behind the bar. His expression seems blank in the neon under-lightning, but his eyes follow the route of the younger cop. Perhaps this is not out of the ordinary; Steve does not seem too concerned. This hardly has the atmosphere of last night's raid at the video emporium or the undercurrent of impending violence that I witnessed at the bar up the street.

The boy in blue winds his way toward our table, sizes up each man he passes, pauses occasionally to stare one or another right in the eye. Then — to coin an ever-popular phase — our eyes meet. Recognizing me, he falters in his stroll; in a whirlwind of revelation, I clutch at the table.

Time, place, and situation are cards laid out before me. No wonder he rescued me at the video store last night, no wonder he moves more deliberately now, his full attention fixed on this table. Two nights past, I happened upon him in this establishment's sordid bathroom.

His uniform should be as flattering as his jeans were — this man has the nicest buns on the force.

Andrew feels safe and secure. No fear of being arrested for contributing to the delinquency of a boy ten years my junior. This boy-in-cop's-clothing is not about to jeopardize his affiliation with the legal goon squad by hassling the man who will — without a moment's hesitation — point the finger at him.

Kevin, not being privy to my knowledge, grips my leg under the table. I try to pry his hand free, but I could as easily pry the jaws of a werewolf off my throat. Yet, his face is calm as he puffs on his cigarette.

The young cop stops before our table. How nonchalant he is, casting about the room as if we do not exist. Then the head swivels around, and those eyes burn through mine into my brain.

My confidence wavers.

"Our *young* friend should be at home at this hour," he says with a voice of dry leaves skittering across cement. His face is all sharply shadowed planes and angels; the smoke that swirls around his head seems to pour from his dark-void eyes. He taps a long, thin finger once on the table, then turns back into the crowd.

He may acknowledge my stranglehold on his status, but no love is lost. Not even Brett possessed a stare as chilled with loathing.

O

After granting our stalwart guardians of law and order a twenty-minute head start, I help Kevin, who has somehow managed another strawberry margarita, to his feet. We walk — correction, I walk, Kevin definitely staggers — up to a grinning Steve behind the bar.

"Leaving so soon?" He nods at Kevin. "I guess he'll be pliable enough."

I flash a twenty under Steve's nose, then make a move toward the v-neck of his sweater. With the deftness of two nights ago, I abruptly switch targets, shove the twenty down the front of his slacks, and do a quick wrap — two bills would have covered the acreage better.

"Thank you ever so much for your kindness." I give his face — filled with amazement — a light pat. "See you around, Steven old boy."

A guiding hand on Kevin's shoulder, I set my sights on the

front door and burrow through the barrier of patrons.

The vicinity is clear of goon-squad cars. I direct Kevin up the street. He rummages in his pockets for his keys, then straddles the Honda scooter.

"Nonono," I say, pulling the key from the ignition.

"Nonono, I'm not walking," he replies.

It is late and I am not in the mood for a debate. I grab him under the arms, pick him up, and set him down on the passenger's seat. Giving him no reaction time, I climb onto the scooter.

"Where do you live?"

He is trying to light a cigarette, but has the lighter upside down.

"Don't burn the Andrew's clothes, it pisses him off." I confiscate cigarette and lighter. "Where do you live?"

He points in the general direction of Alaska. "That way."

I pull into traffic without much grace: the scooter sputters and jolts. Kevin's arms wrap around me, and he giggles hot breath over my ear.

"Turn left!"

Horns blare as I swerve toward the left turn lane. My pant leg brushes the fender of a moving car. Fortunately, we make the turn without injury to body or attire.

"Right! Right!"

My technique on this rattling deathtrap improves as we wind our way out of the Village toward Nome. The peace of quaint residential sections with antiquated street lamps is shattered as Kevin shouts one impulsive direction after another. His high-pitched giggle rings louder than the whine of the engine when I am forced to navigate a hairpin turn.

"Through the alley! No — that alley!"

Trash and debris flutter in our wake. Water splatters my shoes.

I glance at Kevin. Hands on my shoulders, he leans back, his eyes shut, enjoying the whipping wind. A bump in the alley jars the scooter. He leans suddenly against my back, points left and shouts, "Right! Right here!" then giggles wildly.

I hit the brakes. We skid to a halt. Kevin hooks his chin on my shoulder and gazes at me in total innocence.

"Problem?"

"Where are we going?"

"Home."

"Whose home?"

"Who cares?" He burps and giggles in delight of himself.

"Where do you live, Kevin?"

"Up there." Both arms snap out in different directions.

Oh, if ever there was justification for the switchblade. . . .

"All right," he says between titters. "I promise — really."

"Address, or we sit here all night."

"Don't talk to me like I'm five."

"Don't act as if you're five."

That hit a nerve. He straightens, puts the giggle away, and reconnoiters the area. "See that hill with the light at the very very top?"

I start the scooter, and it strains up the hill. At the top, Kevin directs me to a more-than-posh residence.

"You live here? With your parents?" Andrew is saved from further complications in this sticky wicket.

"I don't live with my parents." Such indignance. "I live over the garage. I'll show you." Our brisk drive has sobered him up a bit too much. He remembers his intentions for this evening.

"It's late—"

"How are you going to get home?" He links his arm firmly in mine. "You at least have to come in and call a cab." Minor sobriety also brings on unshakable logic.

My resistance must be weakening; I follow him.

O

His garage apartment is on the barren side, but more sophisticated than I had anticipated. I expected posters of He-Man and Pee Wee Herman. The prints over the sofabed show embryonic good taste.

Kevin switches on a primitive but decent-sounding stereo, turns, and collides with the open, unmade bed. He forces a giggle. He sidles around the bed, keeping his back to it in an effort to make it just go away. A case of the jitters wears away at the effects of the margarita.

"Would you like a beer? — No, you don't mix beer with margaritas."

"I'm fine." I take a step toward him; he takes a step back and falls onto the bed. The boy is up like a jack-in-the-box. I hesitate. "What's wrong?"

"Wrong?" His voice breaks. "Nothing is — I've never done this before."

I halt in my tracks. Most would find that titillating. Most would find that an invitation to total debauchery.

Well, excuse me, but Andrew is not that much different than most. After all, I am — rather was — only human.

O

Kevin is a quick study. In a few short hours, he manages to master most of the techniques and quite a few of the finer nuances. We commence our umpteenth roll across the bed.

How much energy can a drunken eighteen-year-old possess? How much sex can a dead man survive?

Finally, I pin him down, face to face. His legs wrap around my waist, and for one fraction of a second, I feel the hunger. I nuzzle my face at his throat, yet keep my teeth behind sealed lips. His skin is scorching and smooth, his fragrance clean — with an overtone of garlic. I mold against him, turn my face from his throat, and enjoy the quiet rasp of his faint whiskers against mine. Kevin moans deeply against my forehead, paws at my back then — at last — relaxes.

In a breath, he is asleep. I leave him to dream, safe. Alone.

IV

The lights of town twirl in an ever-widening circle. I spiral skyward, cloaked in the warmth of the past hours with Kevin. I scale the air currents until the town is but a speck of hazy light on the coastline. Freefall! Wings retracted, I spin and tumble to within yards of Kevin's roof. The wings snap open. I float, a feather, above the weathered tiles.

The hunger, a chilled void at my center, invades my adolescent exaltation. I veer toward the Village, the blur of treetops below highlighted by streaks of street lamps. Most of the bars are closed by now, but I know all the popular after-hours places where the selection for a late night snack will be wide and varied.

Perhaps too wide and varied. I am too famished to cope with the dilemma of fragile youth, and the prime Village morsels all have it inscribed on their pretty faces and muscled bodies. What Andrew needs is a collection of boys whose looks are more on the downside. I tip a wing, alter course.

Ahead, the lights thin, the waters of the bay sparkle beyond dark seedy buildings. I know just the place, an underground club that caters to the lower elements of the species.

In spite of the hunger, I cannot resist a quick spin over the bay. I dip and rise with the roll of the surf, being cautious, of course, to avoid any spray of that running water. Andrew wants no scars. Then I soar over waves, ribbon of beach, scarred planks of the wharf toward the flicker of dying neon sign set against the peeling face of an abandoned warehouse. Downstairs dinner waits.

O

To the pulse of techno-disco, I descend the uneven, stained-by-who-knows-what cement stairs, all the while careful not to touch the glistening walls. Whatever slime drips down the warped paneling will be cold and gooey, even to me. An odor too foul for any respectable charnel house wafts around me, mingling with the smell of dead fish from outside.

At the bottom of the steps, a bouncer closely related to the orangutan family guards this fine establishment. With close-set peepers, he gives me the once over. Deciding that I will do — imagine looks like those having that kind of power! —he gestures me inside with a dirty-fingernailed paw. I slip past him, swearing under my breath when the back of my jacket brushes against the door frame.

Turn on some lights and turn off the dry ice machine. Electricity must be expensive and cigarettes cheap on this side of town. Faint fluorescent light outlines the bar; on the opposite side of the room, red spotlights pinpoint two male strippers. A swarm of fireflies, glowing cigarettes exhale clouds of smoke into an already dense fog bank.

Working my way through the patrons, I damn my powerful night vision. No wonder lights are kept low and smoke thick. Such an unattractive group, in such unattractive clothes. I take the only available slot at the bar and face the bartender. Urgh! I did not know Bosco boys were permitted to be so — what is that word? — ugly.

"What'll it be?" the bartender asks. Such a high-pitched voice for such a burly primate.

Strawberry margaritas hardly suit this atmosphere; I rack my brain for something a tad more butch, yet not too deadly.

"Scotch, straight up."

Sneering, the bartender turns away. Excuse me, Airhead. Would you be happier if I ordered arsenic?

What Andrew suffers to avoid the dilemma and to have a substantial meal. Maybe in future, I will satiate myself where I want and leave a trail of my own kind instead of a trail of headless bodies. Think of the brain-time that would be saved — no, think of all the competition that would have to be dealt with. Better stick to the switchblade.

The drink proves a bad choice; unlike the favored strawberry margarita, the scotch stimulates the hunger. My insides squirm with anticipation as if every artery, vein, capillary, and ventricle knows I am surrounded by blood-stuffed bodies. A damp film rises on my forehead — the undead with the cold sweats, what a party — and I gape at the stage to distract myself.

Watching the show does not alleviate my desires. The strippers, one black, one white, shimmy upon their pedestals, the faint red light adding enough highlight and shadow to their muscled arms and legs, bulging chests and washboard stomachs to make even Andrew's mouth do a Sahara Desert. I concentrate on their faces. Both are college boys — Andrew knows that high-cheekboned look. Tuition must be paid one way or another I suppose.

That's it, Andrew, use your brain instead of your crotch. You function better.

If, as I theorize, both are college boys stripping their way through — oh, let me conjecture — dental school, why would they choose this landmark of shabbiness and pestilence? To avoid recognition? Or perhaps they are good Samaritans who wish to give the less fortunate a taste of what the rest of the world craves.

Bad children that they are, my eyes follow the deliberate movement of the black stripper's hand as it reaches down, down — yet farther — to release the velcro between his legs. The bikini disintegrates and floats to the ground. A pale shadow, the white stripper does the same, then teases the fragile strap that holds his bulging G-string in check.

An absurd Busby Berkeley nightmare, the strippers' pedestals begin to move, seeming in the darkness to float across the stage, while each man gyrates to the spasmodic rhythms. The pedestals collide — the strippers are tossed slightly off balance.

But into each other's arms. A little voice in my brain tells me this is probably the climax of the act — in every conceivable fashion. Legs entangling, arms flailing, they undulate against each other. Torturously, they sway to the floor; the music crescendos—

And Andrew turns away before losing what little self-control remains. Goodness gracious me, how the lust surges. The time has come to select a mark and fastfoot it to the nearest — and safest — dark alley for a much-needed feast.

I search the dank room for those who are simply homely

beside the truly grotesque. I do have my aesthetics to consider, even at the point of uncontrollable craving; I cannot have my mark's appearance putting me off my food.

Obese and skeletal, pockmarked and sallow-skinned — bald pates and spiked mohawks, concave chests and bloated beerguts — the patrons of this sewage trench slouch hither and thither, exchange mumbled monosyllables and gulp their firewater. A few — bless their pretentious, blind souls — posture seductively in skin-tight, soiled jeans that have been sanded and torn in the most revealing places. At that table, one has the nerve to reveal a deflated pec; over there, another's too-small muscle shirt has crawled midway up his extended paunch. Scattered accents, remnants of the leather crowd, in iron-studded vests and seatless chaps, glower from beneath their black caps. One or two of their number could be possibilities, but I do not fancy having to manipulate the switchblade around their dog collars.

Still, I manage to choose an even half-dozen from the squalor. That one down the bar is not too pale or too thin; he probably has some blood in him. That one over there, near the stage — his hair appears to have been washed within the last week rather than sometime last year. One of the leather boys after all — no dog collar, an intriguing leather jockstrap instead. Chubby, writhing with the music, has the flush of a well-fed baby; he is definitely a full plate. The obnoxious Indian, shirtless and wearing shorts that showcase all his attributes — if only to shut him up.

Last on the list, but hardly last in my eyes, the tall black-haired boy towering over the crowd is almost an anomaly. Somewhere near the ripe old age of twenty-five, he has already been the pawn of time and fate's cruel ravages. What was undoubtedly a pretty pre-pubescent face is now pocked, pallid, and drawn; hair that was once thick and easy to manage is now thinning and grizzled. Obviously, he has tried to maintain the body and elevate it above skinny tendencies. His clothes speak of quiet desperation: tight mess shirt and thin cotton slacks that conform to every sculpted contour. A homeless child — a touch too disintegrated for the Village and a jot too pretty for this bunch of slobs.

He has taken notice of my scrutiny. He glances away, then back as if to be certain. Tentatively, he smiles, accentuating the emotions tangled behind his crystal blue eyes: uncertainty, hopefulness, fear that my attention is a fluke. The eyes have it, Andrew; you cannot allow diabolical life to further degrade the tormented soul of beauty trapped within that fading shell.

I am about to make my move when hands clamp down on my shoulders, and a torch body molds against my back.

"I know you," a voice declares from behind me.

"No, you don't," without even turning. Don't bother Andrew when he is in the feeding mode, Airhead.

"I've seen you around the Village, Andrew. You work at that boutique . . . ."

My mark assumes a rejected posture as I take a quick peek over my shoulder. Yes, yes, the black stripper who moments ago was riding high on his white clone. I have seen him around the Village as well, but my mind is made up.

I turn back to the tall black-haired boy. I catch a glimpse of his back as he retreats toward the door. The head is bowed, the shoulders slumped, the hands jammed deep into his pants pockets — which adds an uplifting definition to already defined buns. I gulp the rest of my scotch, stand to pursue.

"Johnson's the name," the stripper says, blocking my path. "I saw you watching me dance."

How well will you be able to dance with only one leg, Airhead? I scowl — uselessly. Johnson has set his sights as well; Andrew is the target.

I make a last contact with the black-haired boy's eyes before he departs. Some other night — soon — I will find you and terminate the agony. Andrew never breaks a promise.

"You are Andrew," Johnson states.

For the moment. In a flash I might be a very large, very pissed bat that will claw your eyes out.

"I never thought to see you here," Johnson says.

"Sightseeing." How cruel can Andrew be? "Not entertaining the troops."

Johnson smiles. "Have to pay that tuition somehow. May as well have some fun doing it."

Does Andrew know of what he speaks or not?

"Let me get you another drink. Scotch? Barkeep!" Johnson squeezes up to the bar, forces contact with my more sensitive regions. He smiles lecherous approval. "I've always had an urge to run up against you outside that boutique — away from all those nosey people." His shifts his weight — managing an interesting arrangement of things. "I guess this is my lucky night."

Make it his lucky night, Andrew — lucky, lasting, and lethal.

O

After several more scotch aperitifs, I whisper sweet nasties into Johnson's ear. He rises quickly to the challenge.

On the way to the door, I give these wondrous specimens of humanity a last scan — and stop short. Among the pallor and pockmarks I spot a familiar face. Eyes identical to mine track my path. Johnson presses against my back, urging me on. I glare at him, then turn back to my twin. In that fraction of time, he has lost himself in the herd.

As anxious as I, Johnson forces me through the door and up the slippery steps. His hands crank into over-grope; thoughts of anyone else are skimmed from my mind.

Not one to waste time, Johnson drags me around the corner and through the unhinged door of the deserted warehouse. Shafts of starlight illuminate dust and cobwebs, shattered crates and fleeing rats. A whirlpool of wind animates the scattered leaves and shreds of paper and hums a soothing dirge accentuated by the muffled crash of the surf. Appropriate surroundings for a night with Andrew, but still I am cautious. Although Johnson selects a secluded corner, heavy in the shadow department, for our tryst, I scout the floor for marauding spiders and the catwalks for spying head-hijackers.

Careful with the slacks, Airhead. I snatch them off the ground and fold them over a railing. I am trying to be as courteous to my jacket, but Johnson knows what he is about. I tremble from his passion. The hell with the jacket. Just keep it — and the switchblade — within reach.

Our encounter is short — I am still exhausted from Kevin. Yet I summon such intensity that Johnson does not even realize that the hickey on his throat will never fade.

At the end, when my head is spinning from intoxication, I look into his eyes to find a familiar confusion. Even in their last moment, my marks never really understand what I am or that I have spared them the pain of witnessing the slow death of their beauty.

Shoving my tie into the pocket along with the sated switchblade, I walk toward the warehouse door. I halt, turning back to that dark corner. Leaving Johnson there invites trouble from the head-thief. Yet I am tuckered beyond words. Besides, I have no means of transporting him to a more secluded resting place.

An idea works its way through the haze of my thoughts. You are on the edge of the continent, Andrew. A vast ocean is before you. Maybe Johnson always wanted to see the world; send him out with the tide.

Concentrating on that one thought, I go outside to ascertain that the path from warehouse to beach is void of prying eyes. And halt once more.

Here's a sticky wicket for you, Andrew.

At the edge of the wharf, the tall black-haired boy stares out at the water. I take a step toward him; the planks beneath my feet give him warning. He whirls around, sees me. He is shaking, every detail of his face and slim body speaks of terror. He knows what has occurred in the warehouse; he knows what Andrew is.

I cannot move. I do not know what to do. The solution is too obvious: book passage for him on Johnson's tide to oblivion. Quickly and without ceremony. Yet, some obscure emotion holds me back. I wanted to make this one's final exit the experience of his life. Earlier, when I saw his despair, I wanted to ease it, not cut it short. Besides, tears streak his face, and Andrew has always been a sucker for tears.

"Why did you have to follow?" I mutter. "I would have come back for you."

Fresh tears slide down the ravaged cheeks. He has grasped the implication.

"Get away from me," I tell him. "Get away from me now."

He stands immobile; I cannot decipher whether he is paralyzed by dread or by the promise.

From somewhere within me I summon the strength for a decision that may prove a monstrous mistake. I spin away, and in an instant, transform. I soar past him, out over the waves, then circle back as I climb higher into the sky.

Below, he collapses to the deserted wharf. His sobs rise on the sea breeze. I retreat toward the lights of town.

There will be another night, and the seduction will be as I had planned. Andrew is tired of senseless massacres.

O

Such a night, and it holds yet another chore. Home, back to being as human as I can be, I dig through the paper bags in my kitchen closet. One by one, I salvage the three heads. Taking out the trash has never been one of my favorite activities, but I may as well do it while I am thinking about it.

I briefly study the face of each head before I place it into the garbage bag. A twinge of sentimentality surges. I am certain they would freeze well. Still, I cannot see keeping them around the apartment as trophies.

The convertible top down to keep me chilled and focused, I drive up into the hills. The effects of my repast — blurred vision and a slight reduction in the coordination department — make the journey more than a little perilous. Fortunately, the winding road is deserted and I can navigate along the center line and avoid the sheer cliffs.

Far out of town, I pull the car to the edge of a bluff that has always been a favorite of mine. I like to come here to escape the bustle of college boys and the persistence of the dilemma.

Tonight, I stare over the edge at the turbulent ocean and

watch the rock-weighted garbage bag with the three heads disappear beneath the waves. For a brief moment I think of Johnson. He missed his tide; no free world cruise with the fishies. I close my eyes and allow the tangy scent of the sea to swirl around me.

What the hell. If the head-pilferer wants Johnson's head, he is welcome to it. I am too exhausted to feel threatened. Andrew knows that this town is about ready to jerk the welcome mat from under his feet; let the head-robber give the first tug.

V

I wake up mere seconds after sunset, refreshed and ready for another night. Jumping out of my coffin, I skip to the bathroom — without my bathrobe. A warm sensation of Kevin clings to me as if he had slept curled at my side all day. Fragments of dreams skitter at the edges of my consciousness. Dreamland had only two occupants last day — the child-man and me.

The running water in the bathtub splashes my hand. Swearing, I jump back and stare blankly at the rising steam. The welt on my skin is inconsequential to the vision that reared briefly behind my eyes.

Something else was in Dreamland. Something dark, something streaked with blood. Deadly.

Turning off the water, I return to the bedroom. The telephone on the nightstand seems larger than usual, domineering, urgent for attention. I take a step toward it, tempted to call Kevin. What will I say?

See you at work in an hour.

Lame.

How about:

I dreamed about you, and I think someone killed you, but I am still in a damned good mood, considering the horrible things that have happened this week.

Andrew wonders if it is too early for one small strawberry margarita — just to get him out of the house and through the ride to work.

O

I arrive early in the Village. To kill time, I allow the current of college students to shift me from street to street, storefront to storefront. Still unnerved by that shade of evil in Dreamland, I find the sights stale; even the fair faces and buffed bodies sporting pastel elegance have become bland and mundane. With fifteen minutes to spare, I forge against the undertow and find the wave that will carry me to the boutique.

Loitering in front of the newspaper vending machines, I scan the day's headlines. No further word about the Sleepy Hollow Killer. The auburn-haired druggy and Johnson have yet to be discovered. Nor is there an item about a tall black-haired boy claiming he saw a preppy-type in rather drab clothes transfigure into a bat with a four-foot wing span.

Maybe I have more time in this college town than I thought.

Two minutes before my shift begins. No child-man tugs at the tail of my jacket; no giggle resounds through the noisy street to welcome me. Until the very last second — with the store manager glaring through the plate-glass — I linger. The parade of college students in their high-tech fashions passes by. Kevin does not arrive.

"Where's blondie?" the store manager demands when I walk inside.

"Blondie?" I play at straightening my tie. "Which one of the resident airheads could that be?"

"You know damned well, Andrew." His head juts forward from his shoulders, and I am tempted to tweak his banana nose. "Kevin. He hasn't called to say he's sick or that he'll be late. If he doesn't show soon, he's out. There are plenty of boys on the street who would kill to work here."

Maybe one of them already has.

Andrew, you put those thoughts right out of your head. Go help that lad over there decide between the fluorescent striped and plaid shirts. Fiery sunrises! he should not be caught dead wearing either.

O

Work is no joy, but tonight it is torture. From some distant universe, the customers parade through, demanding colors and styles that I, Andrew, epitome of fashion, have never seen, not even on the latest posture-rock video. Each airhead is possessed of a feeble splendor that vicious time will erode to grotesqueness. I do not feel sorry for them; I do not feel the urge to pull out the switchblade and terminate their agony before it begins. Anyone who treats Andrew like a salesperson deserves to end up wrinkled, bent, and toothless.

Andrew is in a piss-poor mood; stay out of his way.

Then the stunner glides in. Long auburn hair, lithe figure, eyes that project an innocence found only in fairy tales — sound familiar? Simple *deja vu*, or am I being haunted? As I assist this dead ringer of the druggy, I stare at his throat, expecting to see a thin red scar where the switchblade did its work. The only blemish is a tiny mole above the adam's apple. I breathe a sigh of relief; Andrew does not need vengeful ghosts dropping by. I hurry this customer along — but not so quickly that he will not be the talk of the town in his new ensemble.

Thank the moon for breaktime! The halfway mark; two more hours and I can find out where the hell Kevin is. Standing on the sidewalk out front, I contemplate the phone booth at the corner. I am afraid to call, afraid that he will not answer. What would I do then? I cannot run off before the shift is over. If I do have time in this town, I need this job.

I turn away from the phone booth and run chest-to-chest into Steve.

"Andrew old boy!" His hands grip me at the waist, holding me momentarily against him. His smile is lecherous. "Why aren't you in there selling shirts?"

"Steven old boy, even I get a break."

"No doubt." He releases me; his smile tightens. "How's the little boy?" His hand skims my side, up my chest, then cuffs my chin. I am tempted to twist off his fingers — one at a time — slowly. "Lose his head over you?" Laughing, Steve swings past me and wades into the crowd.

With the discarded corpses of the Sleepy Hollow Killer littering the town, airheads should not make dangerous jokes.

"Coming back to work tonight, Andrew?" the store manager calls.

"I still have two minutes." Learn to read your quartz digital.

Andrew should have listened and gone inside while the going was good.

A police car inches through the traffic. Old gray eyes is behind the wheel; the young cop rides shotgun. And observes me with unshielded antagonism. I feign nonchalance. The boy-in-cop's-clothing sneers.

"Your two minutes are up, Andrew," the store manager shouts.

Thank the stars.

O

Fifteen minutes until the midnight chimes resound through my head. I pace through the racks of one hundred percent cotton shirts, do a turn through the chrome shelves of sweaters, posture beside the stacks of slacks — in direct line with the mirrors. I scurry over to the shoe display and run twitching fingers over the fake snakeskin. My other hand is deep in my pants pocket. The quarter for the phone booth bites into my palm.

Countdown — ten minutes at a snail's pace.

Then the last customer of the night wanders in.

A five-year-old memory is set free and for the briefest of moments, I see Brett of the compelling face and stone body standing before me. I have enough on my mind without a retake of that night.

The store manager descends on the man, offering to help him make a quick selection. My vision clears, and I recognize the customer for who he really is — the cruiser — my pseudo twin. The identical round brown eyes ignore the manager and lock onto me. The strong hands skim significantly over a pair of trousers on the table. Then, without a word, the cruiser retreats into the night.

In my mind — as clearly as if splashed with vibrant oils on a life-sized canvas — the dark and bloody image from Dreamland takes form. In the center of a black and violet background, Kevin hangs translucent white, his naked body slashed by rivulets of brilliant red.

O

After three rings and the irritating click of an answering machine, Kevin's giggle vibrates through the phone lines.

Kevin's tied up right now — giggle — Not really. Rope scars the skin — giggle — Leave your name and number — and a recent photo — giggle — I'll get you back — giggle . . .

The machine beeps in my ear. For a moment I am silent. What good will a message do if the head-napper has slashed Kevin to pieces?

A little less morbidity, Andrew.

"It's Andrew. Missed you at work. Wondered what happened to—"

The phone clicks, a muffled rush of air through the lines.

I cover my other ear to block out the roar of traffic outside the phone booth.

"Hello? Kevin—"

A dead silence. Another click, the malicious buzz of the dial tone.

Trapped in the confines of the phone booth, I grip the receiver until the plastic cracks. Around me, the students circle, their voices and laughter pressing. A horn blares; I jump, drop the broken receiver. I fumble with the sliding door, push and pull until I am free. On the sidewalk, all the warmth from the oblivious bimbos buffeting me, I look up into the sky. Andrew knows the fastest way to Kevin's apartment, but what would these children think if I transmuted right before their glassy eyes?

O

I decide to take the car. If my imagination has gotten the better of me and Kevin is at home, how would I explain that I flew over — without a plane?

Retracing the route is no easy chore — especially after last night's madcap journey on Kevin's scooter. Eventually, I park in front of the more-than-posh house.

A gust of wind whispers through the trees; the glow of the antiquated streetlamps shimmers, casts restless shadows. I hurry up the driveway, my hand locked around the switchblade.

The apartment above the garage is dark; the stairs creak under my weight. At the door, I hesitate. This is not right; you cannot fool Andrew. Nevertheless, I knock. A sharp echo rattles my eyeteeth. Standing close to the door, I grip the doorknob and twist it; the lock snaps. I push; the door does not budge. Dead bolt. After a glance around the shadow-weaved yard, I press my shoulder against the door — harder. From inside, I hear the wood of the doorframe splinter. The door swings open.

Beyond caution, I rush inside. I bang my shins on the Honda scooter, on its side just inside the door, and fall. My hands hit the carpet, skid over a patch of something damp and sticky. My nose identifies it: blood; I can't quite distinguish the vintage. Patches small and large riddle the carpet; the fragrance mingles with the prominent scent of Kevin's aftershave.

Pushing to my feet, I do a quick scan. No sign of a struggle. I turn to the bed. No wonder; the child-man never knew what hit him.

The head-stealer had the decorum to cover the corpse with the sheet, but the stains of blood, thick at the source, thin around the edges, clash with the geometric pattern.

I am tired; I want a margarita. I do not want to walk the few paces to the bed and pull back that sheet. Remember Kevin as he was last night, Andrew, when you shared that bed with him. Why torture yourself by looking at the mutilated shell?

You brought him to this end, Andrew. You knew better than to get involved while the head-robber lurked in the shadows. You owe the kid a final viewing.

All right, I'll look. But I won't like it.

The best way to handle this kind of unpleasantness is to get it over with as quickly as possible. Two strides; I grab the sheet and toss it back.

Blazing daybreak! this is disgusting. And more than a little tasteless. The shanghaier of heads, possessed of the sickest sense of humor, has added bodysnatching to his repertoire.

I recognize the body. I should — I inflicted those knife wounds. The slim figure belongs to the auburn-haired druggy. But the head — sewn on with wide, unpracticed stitches — belongs to none other than Johnson, stripper extraordinaire.

Relief sweeps through me, starting at my toes and rising with a dizzying chill to my brain. Kevin may still be alive.

Look here, Andrew. The head-pilferer has left you a note.

I pry the envelope from the corpse's fingers. The note is for me all right; my name is scrawled in someone's blood. I pull out a piece of stationary with Kevin's initials at the top.

"Have a margarita — strawberry, of course — your favorite. Relax. We'll meet before bedtime.

"P.S. The little boy has a nice throat."

I shove the note into my pocket, jerk the sheet back over the body, and dash for the door. Andrew can read between the lines. It's time to hit Steve's bar.

At the door, I falter. Blood covers my hands. Twisting my head, I can see faint stains on my shirt. Unless I want to draw undue attention to myself — something Andrew never wants to do — I had better go home and change. While I am there, I will bolster myself with the revolver stashed under my pastel socks — and grab that extra box of silver bullets — just in case.

O

The usual trim bodies and bright faces pack the barroom. I work my way through the haze of smoke and fumes of liquor toward the bar. Over the din of voices, I hear the blender whir to life. By the time I reach the bar rail, Steve has set up a double strawberry margarita. I force a smile of thanks, reach for my wallet.

"My treat," Steve says. He surveys the crowd. "Still alone?"

"Kevin is someone else's captive audience tonight."

I sip the red froth — not too quickly. I cannot get inebriated. I may need all my faculties before the dawn of this night. "Do you have any cigarettes back there?"

Steve slaps a fresh pack and a book of matches onto the bar beside my drink. "Those things will be your death." He walks the length of the bar toward an impatient patron.

Too late to worry about that. I light a cigarette, lean back against the bar rail, and search the milling boys. One of them is the head-burglar. I reach inside my jacket. Yes, Andrew, the revolver is still there, no need to pull it out to check your ammo — six silver bullets ready and waiting. I take another swallow of my margarita. I wish werewolves were my only worry.

My twin the cruiser cruises in and spots me. He really should have that hand examined; it spends a great deal of time hovering over the front of his clingy cotton slacks.

Andrew, stop to consider this one for a moment. I have been seeing the cruiser around quite a bit lately — he was even at the dockside sleaze club. I stub out my cigarette. He could have easily followed Johnson and me — as the tall black-haired boy did — into that warehouse. He had ample opportunity to snatch Johnson's head. If I want a suspect for the purloiner of heads, I could choose worse than the cruiser.

My train of thought has a short trip.

The legal goon squad is on the prowl and has decided upon this bar as their prime objective. Led by old gray eyes and the boy-in-cop's-clothing, a dozen uniformed clones plow through the front door.

"Sonofabitch!" Behind me, the neon under-lighting of the bar casts a grim expression on Steve's face. The eyes are pale with anger. A clawed hand reaches under the bar, resurfaces gripping a sawed-off baseball bat.

Just what Andrew needs, a battle with the police. And a battle there will be. The faces around me darken as the bashers in blue forge their way into the room. These boys, all well lubricated — pardon the expression — will not stand frightened statues while the blue bullies trample over them.

A billyclub flashes above the crowd; a hand grabs it and twists it back. The scuffle has begun. The cops push the patrons one way; the patrons shove the cops back. Action, reaction. How simple; how badly timed. Don't these airheads know the child-man's life is at stake and Andrew cannot get involved in a major uprising?

The brawl surges through the room, catching me in its whirlpool. I am dragged away from the bar, thrust into the path of a thrashing billyclub. I snag the assailant's wrist and look into the eyes of the young cop. The eyes narrow; he tries to pull free. Andrew is much stronger. I jerk him to me. For a fragment, we stand pressed chest-to-chest — and other-things-to-other-things. He likes it — I feel these things — deep down.

I resist a grope at his delectable buns.

"Time to choose sides," I tell him. He struggles, we are forced closer together. He cannot control himself, and I grab him. "Bathroom trysts are going to be difficult to come by after tonight," I warn. "Choose."

I release him. Isn't he lucky that in the fracas no one can see his excitement? He stumbles back, lifts the billyclub.

"Hit me with that, and I'm going to be sorely disappointed."

He falters. The angular face reveals a glimmer of humanity under the blue hat.

Then we are separated, the small gap between us jammed with grappling cops and boys. I hear his billyclub fall to the floor.

Hands clamp onto my shoulder. "The little boy is hanging around at your favorite cliff." A hot breath against my ear.

The hands thrust me into the melee. I crash against the bar rail. By the time I recover, I am again surrounded by the ruckus and unable to identify the head-thief.

Riots in the streets. The insurrection in the bar has spilled out onto the sidewalk, taking Andrew with it. The night is filled with screaming sirens, furious voices, crackling glass. Blue terrorist reinforcements flood the Village. From the other bars, men and women counter-attack. Stonewall reborn, and Andrew has to hit the road.

I dodge through the wrestling adversaries toward the nearest alley. From out of nowhere a cop, his face a snarling death mask, leaps at me. With one hand, I grab his shirtfront and toss him over my shoulder to the other side of the street.

Andrew has no time to play.

I reach the relative calm of the alley, and pause. From the street comes the glow of flame. A fire — I love a good fire. But first things first. I gear up for the transmutation.

A tall figure rushes into the alley — the young cop. I must have made a good impression.

I would love to stay and chat, but I have been cast in the uncomfortable role of hero and must be off.

I race toward the other end of the alley. The young cop's footsteps echo after me. I have speed on my side. I dash into the next street at about fifty, then release my full capability. Let the boy in blue match that without his squad car.

At the parking structure, I wind my way up to my car. I hate to waste time with such humdrum transportation, but I will need to get Kevin back to town. I cannot very well carry him in my claws.

O

The headlight beams of my car flash over the twisting road into the hills, slice across the black boles of trees, stab through the void beyond the ragged-edged cliffs. How closely the head-napper has observed me to know my favorite place of seclusion. How he must dislike me to defile that sanctuary by taking Kevin — hopefully alive, hopefully not too mutilated — there. He might as well have chopped up Kevin and nailed the pieces to the walls of my apartment.

I barely navigate a hairpin curve and top the highest ridge. I stop the car. The road winds down along the cliffs, through a grove of trees, then up again to the bluff. Beyond, the glimmering ocean melds with the star-laden sky.

I can find no sign of Kevin or the head-robber on the narrow bluff or around the crowded trees. Lighting a cigarette, I squint through the smoke. Some detail of the bluff is not right. Something has been added to the landscape, a small alteration that my enhanced vision cannot quite isolate.

I drive down into the grove of trees, park the car in the deepest shadows, and take to the sky. Sure, a bat of my proportion could be easily spotted, especially by someone as observant as the head-pilferer; I hope that by a seaward approach I might gain the advantage of surprise.

Low to the treetops, I wing a circle past the bluff, drop along the face of the cliffs, then glide out over the waves. I glance back, note a peculiar white highlight against the rock wall. Returning my attention to my flight path, I screech and veer sharply to port. Gaping jaws snap out of the water, almost nip a wing. The dull gray body slips under the waves, the high dorsal trailing water.

At a safer altitude, I soar for a pass near that peculiar highlight. Apprehension wells as I draw near. The white highlight comes to definition as a head. Closer. The head is connected to a body. Closer. By the wrists, the body sways at the end of a rope hung over the edge of bluff. I sweep past — the ultimate close-up — and hiss revulsion. The counterpart of the body I found in Kevin's bed: Johnson's body with the auburn-haired druggy's head sewn on at the neck.

Topping the edge of the bluff, I do a low sweep of the narrow clearing. The alteration of the bluff's landscape is the rope from which the body hangs. I follow the rope into the trees, hoping it might lead me to Kevin. The trail stops at a gnarled oak around which the rope is tied.

Frustrated, I change back to human form. Haven't I warned you about concentration, Andrew? I shake my right wing until the membrane folds to a satisfactory semblance of my arm.

Shafts of moonlight quiver through the stirring branches. The surf thunders and echoes, concealing even the crunch of my footsteps. Revolver in hand, I creep through the trees. The head-shanghaier was no fool in choosing this rendezvous site. An army could move about freely in these woods without being seen or heard.

He is here — the head-snatcher. The smell of a familiar aftershave, the fragrance too adult to be Kevin's, wafts with the scent of the ocean and the odor of decaying leaves. Pressed against a tree, I sniff the air. The breeze shifts direction, and I cannot pinpoint the head-pillager's location.

Ever more cautious, I steal toward the bluff. I look low, then high. Yes, look high, Andrew. You were given the decisive clue, and you ignored it.

Bound and gagged, squirming like some monstrous cocoon about to burst open, Kevin dangles from the branch of a tall tree. The last three missing heads, suspended by the hair, keep him company. Seeing me, Kevin stops struggling. Twirling slowly at the end of the rope, he glares down at me. He grunts through his gag; I know obscenities when I hear them.

What does he know now that he did not know last night?

I am struck on the back of the head. The blow is more irritating than painful, but the shock thrusts me out onto the bluff. The revolver is jarred from my grasp. The weapon thuds across the dirt. I turn toward my assailant, seeing the flashing arc of a billyclub. It smacks against my temple, driving me to the ground. Then the sonofabitch head-stealer has the gall to step on my back as he darts past.

Near the edge of the bluff, the head-burglar snatches up my revolver. Triumphant, he turns to face me.

Andrew, you have let your lower anatomy rule you for too long. Just a touch of brain power would have figured this out days ago. He knew you in the old days, when the sunlight was your domain. And he has been around, popping up when least expected, since you took over the night.

Blond hair stirring around his smooth, moonlit face, Steve examines my revolver. He takes out the clip and chuckles at the silver bullets. Snapping the clip back, he levels the revolver on me as I pick myself up.

Steve sneers. "Only you would load a gun with silver bullets."

"Werewolves, a phobia of mine. What's the story, Steve?" I glance toward the woods. How much can Kevin see; how well can he hear? "I'm sure it's been a laugh riot, but can't you find a better hobby than collecting heads?"

"Don't go moral on me, Andrew old boy. I'm not the one with the teeth and switchblade." He fiddles with the revolver, tipping it at my head, at my chest. "You've gotta be stopped. Your kind always do."

Nice attitude if your name is Van Helsing.

"Think of all those men out for a good time with a pretty boy in fancy clothes. They ended up so much chopping-block meat." He has picked his target; the barrel levels at my chest. His finger twitches on the trigger. "You should have gone after the cops that harass us — even an occasional straight man."

"Most straight men have no style."

A rough, humorless chuckle. "You've always had to have the cream of the crop. Even in college, only the choicest morsels for Andrew. Why couldn't you leave us alone and satisfy yourself with the others?"

"Would you sleep with an elephant?"

"Excuse me?"

I thought that might be a bit abstract, Airhead.

"I have no more choice about my marks than you have about who tucks you in at night. Would you switch to the lace and skirt crowd to please the evangelist on the campaign circuit?"

"You do kill people, Andrew old boy."

"You would kill a cow to eat, Steven old boy."

"I'm a vegetarian."

You're a haughty little bastard is what you are.

This argument is futile. Steve is capable of only one perspective. If you do not like the appetite of the undead bloke up the street, stake him to the floor and sleep in righteous peace.

"I have a swell idea, Steve." I edge forward; Steve's finger tightens on the trigger. I wonder if his aim is any good. Would it have to be at this range? "Why don't we get Kevin out of that tree and call it a night?"

"I can't let him go. He knows who I am."

"Turn off the television mentality. We'll tell him it was a game — a joke on Andrew old boy. He has a twisted sense of humor. He'll giggle his pants wet."

"You're not flying away from this." Steve looks toward the trees. "It's too bad about the kid. I needed bait. He was perfect." He glares at me. "It made me sick to encourage you. But I couldn't break the locks on your coffin. I had to get you out in the open, away from the hustle and bustle."

"You can't kill him, Steve." Try this on. "You'll be as bad as I am."

Worse actually. I have never played jigsaw puzzle with the

heads and bodies of my marks. That takes a special brand of dementia.

He shakes his head. Stubborn sucker.

I make the obvious move and lunge.

Steve pulls the trigger — twice — thrice.

The impact thrusts me back a step. The slugs tunnel through me, a tingling pressure like a splinter under a toenail. Two shoot out my back, the other lodges against my spine. Great, I'll limp my way through eternity.

Damnation — look at the holes in this shirt. Isn't this shirt new, didn't I put it on not two hours ago? My jacket is ruined, too. I look up at Steve. Yes, he knows he has really pissed me off this time. I advance.

Steve pulls the trigger again. Confusion, fear distort his face. "But — silver bullets—"

"Are for werewolves. Tinseltown has always confused the two species. Unless you have a handy wooden stake or you can open the drapes to let in the daylight, I'm damned indestructible."

Panic time for Steve. He backs toward the edge of the bluff; I follow. I feel sorry for him. He thought he was doing the right thing. From the look on his face, he wishes he had left well enough alone. As much as I hate it, I reach into my jacket pocket for the switchblade. I don't really want to kill him, but survival, after all, is instinctive.

The ground under his feet crumbles; dirt and pebbles cascade toward the water and rocks below. Steve glances over his shoulder. He sways slightly. I reach for him; my hand brushes his shirt. He jerks away. And falls.

So shoot me again; I dive after him. Instant metamorphosis. My claws clamp around his arm. I flap my wings with all my strength. He has built up too much momentum; I cannot stop his fall. I manage to slow him down, and he crumples onto a rock in the middle of the tide.

I circle. Steve, considerably madder for the experience, swears gibberish, then dives into the water. He swims against the churning waves. I veer toward the top of the bluff. By the time Steve reaches dry land, I will have Kevin out of that tree and back to town.

O

"Hold still or you are going to fall." Straddling a nearby branch, I hold Kevin aloft with one arm. I cut at the rope with the switchblade. Not knowing Andrew's strength, Kevin shakes his head frantically. The rope snaps; Kevin moans. I hoist him onto the branch next to me and sever his bonds.

Tugging the gag out of his mouth, Kevin edges away from me. "Did you and your friend have fun playing life-and-death struggle? I didn't. This tree is uncomfortable. Do you know how long I've been hanging up here?" He consults his superhero watch. "Seven hours! Froze my butt off." He pulls up his shirt sleeve. "Rope burns! Look at that!" He thrusts his arm at me, thinks twice, and recoils. He bumps his head against a disembodied one. He hooks a thumb at it. "Friend of yours, no doubt. I think you owe me an explanation, Andrew. A long, detailed explanation. Don't just stare at me with that goofball look on your face."

The mouth wants some answers.

"Wouldn't we be more comfortable on the ground?"

"Sure, but—"

Hell, as they say, is for children.

I wrap an arm around his waist and jump. Kevin screams. It is quite a drop. We soft land. Eyes squinted, mouth working, Kevin pulls free. He jabs a finger at me, but I don't think he knows where to begin.

"Your shirt is full of holes." He stabs a finger through one and pokes my chest. "Your chest is full of holes!"

"Don't I know it." Straining, I examine the shirt. I am going to need a new wardrobe after this week. I wonder how my credit stands.

"Just forget it, Andrew. I'm history." He takes a few awkward steps toward the road. "You're an enigma I don't even want to begin to understand." He pauses to massage his thigh, then labors on.

"Want a lift?" I ask. Insincerely.

"I'd rather crawl."

Good. I won't have to listen to you piss and moan all the way back to town. I knew he had to have some flaw. Thank the sunset I found out now. Can you imagine putting up with that mouth — and that giggle — for the next three or six millennium?

I take to the sky. Below, I see Kevin, already tired and pouty. I suppress the urge to dive over his head and really scare him. If he is lucky, Steve will be along soon. They are perfect for each other. In my book, temperamental is as bad as schizophrenic.

O

Life is no night flight of panoramic vistas and sparkling starfields. Sometimes a little diversion — like a psychotic bartender who collects heads — makes you take stock and discover that what you think you need is not necessarily what you want. Crazed? Perhaps — but Andrew has been dead over six years, and the brain atrophies, even with a constant supply of fresh blood.

O

Andrew never breaks a promise, someone once said. I think it might have been me.

The underground club at the docks is packed with the usual crowd. There is a new stripper. I don't suppose Johnson, in his present condition, would be too appealing, even to this lot of lovelies.

Tall, black hair shining, my choice slouches at the bar, sipping from a longneck and scanning the room once every twenty seconds. He spots me in the doorway. The pale, pocked face brightens with uncertain relief. Giving no encouragement, I walk outside. He must make his own decision.

The seabreeze is refreshing, and I venture to the edge of the wharf to watch the surf. I breathe deeply of the salt air, close my eyes to the pounding rhythm of the waves. A sensation of warmth surges through my body as the tall black-haired boy wraps his hand around mine. His shoulder presses against me. For a long time, we stare out beyond the edge of the continent.

Naked and cold, I sit on the beach, the black-haired boy cradled in my lap. Patiently, I wait for the alteration to be complete. We had a good time, and I forgot about the switchblade. I trace the arched eyebrow, his cool temple. Respiration returning, he opens his crystal blue eyes. He smiles at the first taste of his new perceptions.

Andrew is faced with a new dilemma.

Where am I going to find a good twenty-four-hour coffin shop?

FANTASYLAND

Brock Stryker had blond hair — but the talk around town (and the town did talk) was that until that incident two years ago, his hair had been brown. Brock Stryker had been fourteen when drunken rednecks decided that his hair, parted off center and swept back from his forehead in two perfect, straight wings, was too "pretty" for a boy. The drunks had pinned him down in the alley behind the Brawlin' Bar and chopped at Brock's hair with their pocketknives.

A few folks witnessed his flight home, and the town was soon prattling stories of Brock Stryker's punk haircut. But it was worse than punk. Brock's only recourse was Mr. Johnston's electric barber shears. In five minutes, Mr. Johnston buzzed down the uneven spikes; Brock Stryker emerged from Johnston's Barber Emporium with a quarter-inch-long brown flattop.

When the hair grew back, it came in blond, and the town

talked of peroxide and L'Oreal. Brock paid no heed; the sun and his mother's genes were his only beauticians.

The blond Stryker boy had a gruff voice for a sixteen-year-old, and ever since the hair incident, the town often commented that he wore the expression of an old suspicious skinflint. If the town spoke to the boy, he would rumble a curt greeting then continue his lone walk from home to school to the grocery store where he worked two hours each evening. The boy's eyes were always distant, the town noted, as if he saw things the rest of the town did not. Brock Stryker, quoth the town, was off in fantasy land.

And so Brock Stryker was.

O

The clouds hung low in a leaden gray sky and cast a thick drizzle across the cobblestones. The young man, his blond hair matted, tugged his Inverness coat tighter and continued his lone walk through the London streets. His cane thudded rhythmically against the cobblestones.

The dripping cemetery gateway materialized from the hazy evening. The young man stopped, his brown eyes scanning the disarray of headstones beyond the gate. After that brief hesitation, he grasped the cold wet iron, and pushed the cemetery gates open. He had an assignation in this place, and no hulking gravestones would keep him from it.

A dense fog had taken possession of the cemetery. The haze weaved through the squat stones, the small tombs, the tall angelic statues. The mist circled the young man, caressing his hand, nuzzling his cheek, smoothing his damp blond hair. Steadfast, he marched toward the massive mausoleum at the back of the cemetery.

His meeting was to take place here.

He did a turn through the plots before the mausoleum, coolly surveying the vicinity for places of concealment, points of ambush. But he was not worried. He jabbed the end of his cane into a fresh mound.

"Very kind of you to be punctual, Master Stryker." The voice with its crude American accent came from the left.

Dislodging his cane, the young man turned with deliberate calm to assess his adversary. The man was middle-aged, hair thin and receding, beard unruly. The pale eyes squinted out of a drink-bloated face.

"You have, of course, the jewel," the man said, descending the mausoleum steps.

"I have. And my friend?"

The stout man extracted a hand from the pocket of his great coat. A sheaf of curly hair hung from between his fingers. Beads of mist clung to it. "He is here."

The young man bit back of growl of rage. Glaring at the stout man, he reached inside his coat. He held out a small leather pouch. "The jewel."

"Let me see it," the bearded man demanded.

"Let me see my friend."

The bearded man chuckled. "First, you have to dig him up. Provided I remember whose name we buried him under."

The young man gripped his cane. He stepped forward.

"Alive, of course," the stout man said. "Supplied with air through a hollow reed." He released the strands of hair; they drifted to the mud. He extended his hand, fingers flexing. "The jewel."

The young man tossed the leather pouch. The man's pudgy fingers were clumsy. The pouch struck the mausoleum step with the faint shatter of glass.

The American frowned at the pouch. "A trick, young Master Stryker." He gloated. "I am forced to plug that reed."

The rage broke unchecked. The young man gripped his cane in both hands and jerked his sword from the wood scabbard. Brandishing the weapon, he lunged at the stout, bearded American. Thunderstruck, the man stumbled back, lost his footing on the slick stone steps, toppled backward. His head struck the wall of the mausoleum.

The young man towered over his fallen adversary. Stunned, the man squinted up at him. The young man placed the tip of his sword against the flab of his enemy's throat.

"Tell me where he is, or I shall run you through."

"My men will have your scalp for this," the man choked.

"Tell me!"

The sword tip drew blood.

"You were standing atop him."

The young man glanced back at the fresh mound, then down at the stout man. "You diseased bastard. You don't deserve to live." The urge welled to shove the blade home. The young man forced himself to step back. "Get out of here. And stay clear of my friend and me. We know who you are now. I shan't be so merciful next time."

The American hoisted himself to his feet. A hand swiped at the trickle of blood on his throat. His brow furrowed; his lips parted.

"Threats are meaningless," the young man said. "You played your hand and lost. In this country, a gentleman puts his losses behind him. Be off."

With a final glare, the stout American strode past the young man and around the crooked gravestones.

A pick and shovel were hidden just inside the mausoleum.

Snatching them up, the young man hurried to the fresh grave. He took a moment to locate the hollow reed, to clear back dirt and pooling rainwater. "I am here," he said close to the small air hole and wondered, as he began to dig, if his friend had heard.

After five minutes, he was sweating. He tore off his Inverness coat and dinner jacket, the pocket heavy with the real jewel. While the chill drizzle soaked his shirt, he dug, fighting exhaustion, panic, reminding himself that his friend could breathe.

He tossed aside a shovelful of dirt. Air caught in his throat. The young man froze.

Three feet down, the hollow reed was broken and filled with wet dirt.

O

Panic attacked, swelled from his bowels. Locked muscles turned liquid. The shovel slipped from his hands. He collapsed to his knees in the shallow hole, dug frantically at the moist dirt clogging the pipe.

A hand came down on his shoulder. "Brock?"

He flung off the hand, scraped the dirt out of the pipe. "Brock!"

No! Leave me alone! He can't get air!

He was grasped by both shoulders, pulled back from the pipe. He struggled, sound breaking in his throat.

"Brock, what's wrong? Son—"

He jerked around, stared up at his father's concerned faced. Behind his father, his mother, her hands dripping dishwater, watched. Her eyes were filled with fear.

"Are you all right?" his father asked.

Brock managed a nod. But he was not all right. The hollow

reed was broken; his friend could not breathe.

"Come out of there, Son." His father took his hand, and Brock let him hoist him out of the hole.

The cemetery was his backyard, the mausoleum his house. Droplets of water splashed lightly on his face. The London fog was the lawn sprinkler.

Brock looked back into the hole. In a shadowed corner was the broken pipe — the septic tank pipe. Beside the hole was the sapling he had been planting.

"Why don't you come in out of the heat?" his mother suggested. She glanced nervously at his father.

"Yeah," his father said. "I'll get you a beer."

"No, I'm all right." Brock forced a smile, but the worry on his parents' faces was not easily diminished. "I want to stay out here."

He glimpsed the broken pipe. He had to get back to that cemetery in London. His friend could not breathe.

O

Slinging his backpack over his shoulder, Brock walked out of Gabbler High School's cool hallway into the warm spring air. Other students milled around him, but none spoke to him as he did not speak to them. Their voices and laughter blared in his ears.

At the end of the sidewalk was a group of boys. He recognized each of them from one or another of his classes, but only one of the boys held his attention.

Charley Donovan.

Tall, loose blond curls, hazel eyes, thick lips.

Charley Donovan was looking at him as he passed. A sidelong, tentative look. Brock bowed his head an instant, then glanced back. Charley Donovan was still watching him with those hazel eyes. A trace of a smile accentuated the lips.

Brock walked on.

Charley Donovan.

O

The black night pressed at the fringe of the firelight. From beyond the cave entrance, rumbling roars and piercing shrieks, highlighted by an occasional phrase of flute-like birdsong, filtered through the jungle.

The young man sat cross-legged near the jittery flames. He contemplated adding more dry vines to the fire, but dawn was not far off. He and his companion would leave the cave at daybreak to search for an escape.

He only hoped the cutthroats who had stranded the two of them in this African jungle had departed.

From behind him came a muttered oath. His companion stirred in his sleep, his hand working fitfully. Was he, in his dreams, still engaged in the futile struggle? Did he yet fight for possession of his cutlass? Perhaps in the dream, the tables would turn and all would not be lost.

The young man looked out beyond the dying fire. The first gray mist of dawn crept through the black night.

His companion would wake, the dream would end, and their situation would still be desperate.

The day before, they had been mates on a privateer, but the vagaries of the captain's foul temperament had turned against them. A misspoken word, and the captain had drawn his cutlass. A big man, the captain had driven the young man against the fife rail. The fight had seemed decided in the captain's favor when a third cutlass entered the fray.

The young man looked back at his sleeping companion.

If not for the crew's intervention, the reading of the ship's rules by the quartermaster, he and his companion would have both died by the captain's cutlass. Instead, they had been marooned on the African coast, at the mercy of the jungle.

"Did you sleep at all?" His companion was kneeling beside him. "Or did you keep watch all night?"

"I slept off and on."

"Liar." His companion sat beside him. Their shoulders touched. "You've been awake all night. Keeping watch. Replenishing the fire."

The young man stared into the jungle, the depths detailed in the growing light.

"You could have wakened me. I can take my own turn," his companion said.

"I couldn't sleep anyway."

"Do you think they've gone?" his companion asked after a moment's silence. "Or do you think he's still arguing for our execution?"

The young man shrugged, then stood. "It's light enough. We'd better get moving."

"To where?" The firelight cast bright points in his companion's hazel eyes, lightened his blond hair.

"Up the coast. Away from here." He offered his hand and hoisted his companion to his feet. "Maybe there's a settlement or something."

His companion surveyed the jungle. "Who'd settle here?"

"We mustn't waste time."

After smothering the fire, the young man led his companion into the jungle. During the night, the jungle seemed to have grown over the path they had broken from the coast the day before. Liana vines and thick ferns blocked their way;

treacherous brush hid rotting logs that tripped them.

Around them rattled the sounds of the jungle. The squawk of birds, the distant roar of some predatory cat, the bellow of apes nearly drowned the crash of the surf.

They finally reached the edge of the jungle. Cautious, the young man restrained his companion within the shadows. He scanned the strip of beach, the rolling waves, the ocean. The privateer schooner was not there.

"They've left," his companion said, relief in his voice. "We may be marooned, but at least we're alive."

"But for how long, maties?" came a heavy voice from behind them.

The young man grabbed his companion's arm, dragged him out onto the beach, then spun around.

A wicked grin slashing his scraggly beard, the stout captain stepped out of the jungle shadows. "I'll flay you both — piece by piece — from the hair on your heads to the soles of your feet." His cutlass flashed in the bright sunlight.

O

A soiled baseball cap pushed back on his head, the stout man stepped out of the Brawlin' Bar and onto the sun-dazzled sidewalk. A pool cue dangled in one hand. Scratching his beard, he looked around, paused, grinned.

From across the street, Brock stared at the man.

In the tangled streets of the town there was no escape. Around every corner the fat man and his beer-reeking friends waited with foul words, pocketknives, and more crude weapons.

The other men from the bar were gathering behind the bearded man. They all saw Brock, and their pale faces twisted with corrupt mirth as they pointed, whispered, and laughed.

Brock backed away. He was stranded without a weapon. He turned to run and collided with Charley Donovan.

An awkward moment, Brock met Charley Donovan's startled gaze. Hoarse laughter from across the street buffeted Brock, shattered his paralysis.

"I'm sorry," Brock said after a backward glance at the bar. He knelt to pick up Charley's fallen school books.

They grabbed for the same book. Charley Donovan's fingertips grazed the back of Brock's hand.

Why here — in the center of town — with my enemies watching?

Still, he could not look away from Charley Donovan's face. And for a moment, it seemed Charley Donovan could not look away from his.

"Are you boys okay?" Mr. Johnston, hair scissors in hand, asked from the doorway of his barber emporium.

Charley Donovan's face blanched, then flushed with embarrassment. "Yes, sir," he croaked, fumbling to pick up his books.

Brock watched confused. Then he noted Mr. Johnston's curious expression.

Of course. They're all gossips.

Snatching up a last sheet of paper, Charley sprang to his feet.

Nodding, Mr. Johnston returned to his shop.

Brock stood, excited and crushed. For a moment — a bare fragment of time — something exceptional had occurred. He examined the back of his hand.

Charley Donovan's fingertips grazed the back of my hand.

An instant frozen in his memory that he could relive at will.

"Brock." Charley Donovan halted in his flight and turned

back.

He knows my name.

"Maybe I'll see you tomorrow at school," Charley called, then ran up the street.

The exceptional moment returned; Brock felt a smile forming on his lips.

"Brock!" a drunken voice mocked.

Anger burned through him, throbbed behind his eyes.

"Maybe I'll see ya at school!" the stout man shouted. In the doorway behind him, his henchman laughed.

"Maybe I'll see you boiled in oil, my fat, bearded whoremaster," Brock whispered. He turned toward home.

○

A dry ocean of undulating tall grass, the land stretched flat to the stark precipices of the mountains. Overhead, the sun glared in a white sky. A breeze mingled the clean smell of the grass with the strong odor of the mammoth beasts that grazed on the plain.

The youth crouched low in the scratching grass. Sweat trickled off his body from the dry air and burning sun. Alert to the milling beasts with their long, curved tusks, he crept toward the mountains. He carried a heavy, gnarled branch.

The youth halted, sniffing the air. A shift of breeze had brought another scent. Tensed, he searched the plain. Only the beasts were in view. He moved on. The scent grew stronger. He paused again, peered over the high grass.

Something brushed against his hand.

Jumping aside, he swung back his club.

Poised defensively, another boy, long, curly hair stirring in the breeze, gaped at him through the blades of grass. He carried no weapon.

The youth hesitated. He examined the boy, sniffed surprise and fear. Haltingly, the youth lowered his club. The curly-haired boy relaxed, then edged forward. Wary, the youth leaned forward, lifted a hand.

A roar echoed across the plain. The ground rumbled.

One of the beasts, head lowered, tusks gleaming, charged across the plain.

The youth grabbed for the boy's arm. His fingers slipped over sticky skin. Long hair flashing in the sun, the boy dashed toward the distant forest, not looking back. The youth started to follow, but the beast's advance blocked the way. The monster bore down on the youth. He raced ahead of it, twisting, turning through the tall grass. He tried to veer toward the forest, after the boy, but the beast halted, then charged again, pursuing the youth across the plain toward the mountains.

O

The shaggy animal pounced, thudded against his side, and knocked Brock breathless to the ground. He lay stunned. The gargantuan face of his neighbor's Saint Bernard loomed over him. With its huge tongue, the dog lapped at Brock's cheek.

"Nice mutt," Brock said hoarsely.

"Stop teasing Angeline!" his neighbor shouted gratingly. Six-foot-four, Widow Grimstone, as thin as the porch posts, stood on her front step. "Brock Stryker, I've told you not to pester that poor old girl. Angeline! Here, old girl!"

The Saint Bernard gave Brock a farewell kiss across the mouth, then bounded over him toward Widow Grimstone.

Dragging the tail of his t-shirt over his face, Brock picked himself up.

"I'm going to talk to your mother, Brock Stryker, if you

bother Angeline again." The widow patted Angeline's head. "I won't treat you like crystal just because some thugs took pocketknives to your hair. I'll talk to your mother *and* your father."

"Your damned dog attacked *me*!" Brock shouted.

Widow Grimstone straightened to full, towering height.

"Keep the mutt on a leash or I'll call the dog catcher!" Defying the widow's pale rage, Brock turned and marched half a block before glancing back. Saint Angeline sat panting on the widow's porch; Widow Grimstone was pounding on his parents' door.

"They'll know better," Brock whispered, walking toward downtown. "Mom says you're a bossy old crone and your dog's a wild beast."

He checked his pocket, hoping he had not dropped the money and the list his father had given him. Feeling the crumpled paper, he smiled. Off to the hardware store and not back to the vengeful talons of Witch Grimstone.

O

It was late Saturday afternoon and downtown was deserted. The town was either at home watching singing hillbillies on television or hanging over its collective gossip fence, assessing the week's events. No one to watch or harass him, no one to judge or persecute. Brock kicked a rock along the sidewalk and whistled a short refrain.

A deserted town was the best town.

Now, if only Charley Donovan were walking up the street from—

Brock halted in front of Johnston's Barber Emporium. Echoing laughter reached him and drew ragged fingernails of apprehension down his back. The raucous noise resounded, digging at a two-year-old memory: murky half-light, liquor-fouled air, dull flashes of knife blades. Sickness seeped from his stomach to his bowels. His legs and arms itched with sweat. His mouth tasted sour, and his eyes burned with incipient tears.

Without turning, Brock knew the evil chuckles came from the alley beside the Brawlin' Bar.

The window of Johnston's Barber Emporium mirrored the afternoon sun, but faint fluorescent light revealed the dim outline of Mr. Johnston, asleep over his newspaper, in his barber's chair.

A single candy wrapper skidded over the asphalt in the breeze. *Crackle . . . . Scratch . . . . Crackle . . . . Scratch . . . .* the only sound besides that laughter on the empty street.

A deserted town is the most terrifying town.

Brock turned toward the Brawlin' Bar.

The small, tinted windows were black slate against the dingy white building. The door yawned open, revealed shadowed depths accentuated by red and blue fluorescence. A single cuetick leaned against the doorframe.

The laughter again — an evil, cackling burst that forced Brock to face the alley entrance. Figures moved through the shadows with a strange erratic fluidity.

They have found some new victim to torture.

What could he do? They had overpowered him before. Nervously, he pushed a strand of blond hair from his forehead. Why wasn't anyone else around? Where were all the nosy, gossiping people of the town when they were needed?

There was Mr. Johnston.

But Mr. Johnston was old. What help would he be against

these villains?

Words drifted from the alley. Words that Brock had heard two years before were repeated by rote.

"Such pretty blond hair for a boy. What boy wants a pretty girl's hair?"

Brock stepped off the curb. Only he could stop the madness.

"Does the pretty boy with the long, pretty hair know a pretty girl's tricks?"

He started across the street. The late afternoon sun waned. Sweating walls of darkness closed around him. A tunnel of dark stone led to the arched entrance of the alley torture chamber.

"Show us your tricks, and we won't cut your pretty hair. Perform your tricks, pretty boy."

Unseen, Brock stopped at the edge of the alley dungeon. The villains were all there, headed by the stout, bearded man. Their prey cowered against the far wall.

Rage swept through Brock, momentarily distorting the alley tableau.

Their prey was Charley Donovan.

The bearded man snapped open his pocketknife. The four-inch blade glinted in a thread of light.

"Perform or—" The man faltered, his head turned slightly. Then he spun around.

Brock tensed, a moment of confusion invading his outrage. Where was his sword?

Wearing black cowls and blood-stained leather jerkins, the torturer and his henchmen advanced.

Brock cast about, desperate. On the ground, by the trash bin, a yard-long piece of one-inch pipe.

"Come to join your friend?" the torturer asked. The mouth

split in a rotted-tooth grin.

His face bruised, blood streaming the line of his chin, Charley was chained to the wall. Before him stood a brazier, iron pikes heating in the red coals.

The torturer gestured his henchmen forward with a flick of the white-hot brand he held. "Let him join his friend."

Brock dashed for the lead pipe.

One of the henchmen lunged, knocked the young man against the rack. The young man clubbed his adversary on the temple, thrust him back.

"Subdue him!" the torturer ordered. "Lash him to the rack!"

The henchmen closed in.

The young man snatched up his sword. The blade lashed out; the villains hesitated. The young man advanced; the villains retreated.

"Idiots!" the torturer roared. "He's only a boy. Subdue him, and you'll each have a turn at him."

Again they attacked, each armed with a pike from the brazier. The young man countered. Iron sparked against iron. Villains sprang from all sides. The young man deflected their assaults; each blow sent painful tremors up his arms to his shoulders. But he would not submit. He parried, twisted round, lashed out. He caught one man off guard; his weapon thudded into the man's side. The man tumbled to the ground.

Rallied, the young man resumed the attack. His sword swung out in endless, sweeping arcs. He forced the villains back, felled another then another. He had bested them; their evil could not withstand his wrath. Another crumbled under the thrashing of his sword.

"Cease or I finish your friend." The torturer's voice reverberated off the stone walls and ceiling of the dungeon. In the quivering light of the brazier, he gripped a handful of his prisoner's blond hair. He poised the fiery tip of the iron brand. "First his hair. Then his face."

The young man clenched his sword, glimpsed his friend, then the torturer. Any sign of hesitation or weakness would mean destruction at the torturer's hands.

The young man charged; the last of the henchmen fled before him, leaving the torturer unprotected. His yellowed eyes wide with disbelief then terror, he tried to lash out with his brand. The young man brought his sword down on the torturer's wrist. Howling agony, the stout man dropped the brand, clattering, to the ground. The sword flashed back. The torturer flattened against the wall beside his victim. Streaking around, the sword slashed into the bearded man's chest. Leather jerkin split, flesh separated. Blood gushed forth. The torturer collapsed to the ground.

O

Every muscle of his body ached; he trembled from exertion. His throat and lungs burned with each breath. His eyes stung.

"Brock?" Charley Donovan's voice, weak and quavering.

Brock looked from the moaning fat man lying in the alley's filth to the lead pipe in his hands to Charley Donovan pressed against the side of the Brawlin' Bar. The chains were gone, but the bruises and trickle of blood on Charley's face remained. His shirt was ripped open; red welts marred his shoulder and chest.

Brock drew in a breath, held it a moment, released it. The pipe slipped out of his hands. He felt relaxed, at ease, somehow cleansed. He stepped over the fat man to stand before Charley Donovan. "Are you all right?" Carefully, he wiped the blood off Charley's chin.

"Yeah." Charley moved away from the wall, stumbled, grabbed at Brock's arm for support. "The bastard kicked me," Charley said, massaging his calf.

"He won't anymore." An arm around him, Brock turned Charley toward the street.

"What in blue blazes—" Mr. Johnston stood at the alley entrance. Five rednecks lay dazed and moaning on the ground between the barber and the two boys.

"Would you call the police, Mr. Johnston?" Brock asked. "These men have been trying to steal your job."

Mr. Johnston clutched at the barber's shears in the pocket of his smock. Nodding, he hurried back across the street to the barber shop.

O

After the second incident behind the Brawlin' Bar, the town remember that Mr. and Mrs. Stryker's only son had been blond as a toddler. The town decided that Brock Stryker's blond hair became him, and talk of peroxide and L'Oreal went down the drain.

Most days after that, Brock Stryker was seen walking to school to home to work with Charley Donovan. The two boys' mingled voices drowned out the town's. Now, Brock Stryker's eyes were focused on sights before him and not some distant place. Brock Stryker had returned from fantasy land.